I0539206

The Tree's Sister

*Everyone has a relationship with nature,
some realize & some don't*

ANKIT SINGH

tulrac

First published in India 2015 by TULRAC
Jodhpur (Rajasthan) - INDIA
Tel: (+91) 9783766121
USA: (+1) 415-376-0036
Email: info@tulrac.com
Website: www.tulrac.com

Copyright © Publishers

All rights reserved. No part of this publication may be reproduced, stored in or introduced into a retrieval system, or transmitted, in any form, or by any means (electronic, mechanical, photocopying, recording or otherwise) without the prior written permission of the publisher. Any person who does any unauthorised act in relation to this publication may be liable to criminal prosecution and civil claims for damages.

DISCLAIMER

This book is a work of fiction. Names, characters, businesses, organizations, places, events and incidents either are the product of the author's imagination or are used fictitiously. Any resemblance to actual persons, living or dead, events, or locales is entirely coincidental.
All disputes subject to Jodhpur, Rajasthan [India] jurisdiction

ISBN : 978-93-5196-430-8

Book editor : Rachana Gehlot
Cover Illustration & Design : Sonakshi Sharma
Inner Layout & Typeset : Ankit Singh

Price : US $7.99 / US $ 1.49 (E-book)
E-Book version available on major online stores

DEDICATION

This book is dedicated to the Almighty God. I also dedicate this book to my grand parents. As their grand-child, I want to imbibe their hard working capabilities, their sincerity & care towards their profession and family.

About the Author

Ankit Singh is a pharmacy-graduate and presently preparing for the prestigious & highly-competitive Civil Services Exam. He has done a certificate course in Medical Transcription from the College of Extended & International Education, California State University, Dominguez Hills (United States of America).

A freelance writer by passion, he likes to read, write and explore new places. He resides in Jodhpur city of Rajasthan(India) which is also known as Suncity and known for its heritage and culture. He can be reached at : ankit@ankitsingh.me

Acknowledgments

First and foremost I would like to thank the **Almighty God**, who let it happen. Then my sincere thanks goes to my parents **Dr. Tulsi Ram Gehlot** & **Mrs. Rachana Gehlot**, who were my first guide and always supported me with my ideas. My mother helped me out as an Editor and so deserves the Editing credits too.

My sister **Kavya**, who helped a lot by reading my manuscript and providing valuable inputs for further improvement of the same.

My special thanks to Singer & Rock-star **Pinky Paras**, who is a very caring person & my favorite singer, too. Her interview about following one's dreams is very motivating & a must-read.

My special thanks to **Sonakshi Sharma**, a talented graphic-designer and a good friend. Her inputs, all through-out the book-making process, helped a lot.

My favourite teacher, **Mrs. Geeta Verma** also deserves special thanks, as she always encouraged and helped us to express our thoughts in a better way. I remember, how she motivated us to write answers in our own words based on our understanding of the chapter, in school. Learning such important things at the school level helps a lot, throughout life.

I would also like to thank my close-friends and family, who directly or indirectly motivated me, to write the book.

Last, but not the least, I would like to thank the Distributors, Printing services providers, and all others involved in the Publishing process.

Prologue

"I think that you should reconsider the decision, mom." – Pratik requested.

"I have already told you that my decision is final. No chance of re-consideration is there in this decision." – His mother replied almost instantly.

Pratik was quite sad with this. He had promised his boss that he will find a suitable place for the office. When his boss came to the city and was interested in his ancestral property, then he was excited to get this offer and thought he would convince his mother for this. But now things were not working as supposed.

"Mom, please try to understand. We will be getting a bulk amount every month just for signing a document. That's it." – Pratik tried for the last time.

"It's a no always. No matter how many times you ask, the answer will be no." – His mother replied angrily in a single tone.

"It will ruin my reputation in front of my boss. He has asked me and I committed him that I will convince my family for the lease. Please try to understand." – Pratik told angrily.

He was in such a position that he had committed in advance about the lease. It was his fault but had put his reputation on stake in front of his boss.

"Don't show your anger to me, Pratik. I am your mother, don't forget this." – His mother replied loudly.

Pratik was a management trainee in a big firm in Australia. He came for the vacations to India, at his home. He was quite happy when his employer Mr. Paul called him and informed him about his interest to take on lease, the front portion of their ancestral house for the construction of their branch office in India. He then thought that it would be easy to convince his *mother as they will get good amount as rent, and so committed him right away, due to which such situation arose.*

"Sorry" – Pratik replied slowly. By now, he somehow realised that it was his fault to commit his boss right away, without his mother's consent.

"It's okay. And, it is your fault. Before committing to anyone regarding this, you should have asked me. I would have refused at then only." – His mother explained.

Pratik got upset. He was wondering why his mother is denying to this. He could not bear the question in his mind and asked, "Mom what is the reason that you are denying to the lease?"

"You know the reason surely. Don't you?" – His mother responded angrily.

Her voice indicated she was angry over being asked the same question again & again. She wanted to end the issue but Pratik was not letting to end the issue. This was making her upset.

Pratik thought for a while, and then replied, "Mom, there is no place for these affections in this era. The front part of the house is a useless part as of now, which can be monetised if we wish to."

"Nothing is useless Pratik. Everything is there for a reason." – His mother replied, before he ended his talk.

Just then the bell rang. The maid went to open the gate. Both of them got silent for the moment.

"My prospects of job in India may also be fulfilled this way. You never know may be." – Pratik said breaking the silence and tried to convince her, once again.

"Why only this property, there are many other properties available in the city. Try asking their owners, but not this one." – His mother replied

They got silent for a while, as the maid had arrived in the room.

"Who has arrived, Shanta?" – Mrs. Shruti Singh asked.

"Madam, Mrs. Asthana has sent her driver to pick you up for the speech. He is waiting at the gate." – Shanta replied.

"The speech will be on which subject and at what time?" – Pratik asked formally.

"Environmental conservation will be the subject. If you intend to listen,

you can come too." – His mother responded.

"Shanta, tell the driver that I am coming in 5 minutes."

"Ok madam." – Shanta, the maid told and went away.

Dr. Shruti although a doctor by qualification, was an environmental lover by passion. She regularly gave speech at various occasions to aware the people regarding Environmental protection and conservation.

"No mom. I am not in mood to attend the speech." – Pratik lies on the bed to take rest.

"Your mother will be delivering the speech. You will have the opportunity to listen to the whole speech sitting in the VIP section." – His mother tried to convince him, as she knew that he is angry over the issue of lease of the land.

"No mom, I don't like such things. Many such campaigns are happening but these things make only a little difference." – Pratik concluded.

"Trying your best is the thing, you can do. Rest is the Almighty's wish." – His mother said

Pratik was trying his best to change his mother's 'No' for the lease of the front land of the ancestral house of his maternal grandparents. But, his mother was stick to her decision.

"Ok, as you wish. I will be attending the whole event today as my speech will be at the end of the event, so I will be late today. Ask Shanta to make the lunch." – His mother told.

"Ok mom. But, please if possible.." – He stopped in between.

"If possible..? What?" – His mother asked

"If possible, please think about the proposal again, mom." – He requested.

His mother didn't say anything and instead said, "You planned to meet your school friends today. Do meet them for sure but come home early in the evening. I have some work to be done." She didn't want to mess up things & so diverted the conversation, instead.

"Okay. But the Boy's party usually continues till late night, so I can't guarantee." – He replied.

His mother by now had understood that he was still upset about her decision for the lease, but she was confident that after spending fun moments with school friends, he will be alright.

She left at the right time for the venue of the event, where she had to deliver the speech. She knew that may be he might change the decision and so left one VIP pass on the table for Pratik too.

On the other hand, Pratik was very much disturbed with the fact that they will lose the golden lease opportunity due to emotional issues of his mother. "Emotions are true at their place. But, cash is the thing that is more valued today" – He thought.

He was unable to understand why his mother is stick on the decision. Emotional bonding with people, places etc are fine to some extent, but when such golden opportunities knock our door, then saying 'No' to them for such things is not a wise thing to do – Pratik thought.

He was in his thoughts, when his phone beeped. He looked up and it was a text message from his school buddy – "Hey Pratik, We will meet at the club @ 4pm"

"Ok. So they will be coming late. I have some leisure time left." – He thought.

"I think I should read some book. Mom has a good collection of books and magazines in her study room. I think I should bring some magazine or book for a time-pass." – He said to himself.

He went to the study room. Shanta Bai, the maid was quite honest at her work and due to this, the whole study room was very much organised. Everything was clean, organised and at its place. Not even a single trace of dust was observed.

He opened the door of the almirah, in which his mother usually stocks the magazines. Usually this is where he finds magazines of his choice – Business and Economy related magazines.

"Oh wow! The current issue of this magazine is the most sought. Mom knows my choice." – Pratik said happily, as he picked one of the magazines of his choice.

He was about to close the door of the almirah when he observed a maroon diary in the top shelf. He got curious and took it in hand.

"Hmm.. It's a personal diary" – Pratik murmured.

He opened the first page and the title "The Tree's sister" was written in a very stylish way using red and golden-coloured glitter pens.

The glittering appearance and the red-golden colour combo as well as the unique name attracted Pratik. It also encouraged him to read further.

He recognized his mother's handwriting and recalled that his mother once told him that she will be writing a book, when he was in Australia.

"Is this the same, mom was talking about?" – He said to himself

"But, the title is somehow unusual – 'The Tree's sister'. How can a tree have a sister?"

Pratik was now curious to know about the book and he turned to the next page.

1

The peon just arrived at the gate of the class room. Class – 1ˢᵗ students began to whisper in low voice with each other. Teacher on seeing this, instructed the students, "No noise. I want a pin-drop silence in the class."

Peon handed a piece of paper to the class teacher, who took a glance to the paper for a while; she signed the same and then turned towards the students. "Listen students. Here is an important announcement to be made." – She said.

The students stopped whispering with each other and there occurred a pin-drop silence in the class. "Tomorrow will be a holiday on account of Rakshabandhan. School will re-open on the day after tomorrow." – The teacher announced.

All the children were excited to hear about this & began whispering in low tone with each other.
"My aunt will be coming on the occasion of Rakhi to our house. I will play with my cousins for the whole day." – Rahul whispered to Mohit.
"I am going to my uncle's house along with my mummy, this Rakhi." – Seema said in a delighted voice.

"My uncle will be coming on this Rakhi from abroad. He promised to bring a lot of toys for me" – Muskaan said delightedly.

"Where will you be going this Rakshabandhan, Shruti?" –

Seema asked Shruti (her classmate).

Shruti got confused. Her mother never told her about Rakshabandhan. She was just thinking it to be a holiday of some kind.

"Do we have to go somewhere on this day?" – She asked curiously.
"Yes. My mother goes to my uncle's house this day to tie Rakhi on his hand, and my aunt comes from Jaipur for the same. Don't you tie Rakhi on your brother's hand?" – Seema said.

"I don't have any idea. I will ask my mother about it." – She replied. She didn't know what to reply, as her mother didn't tell her about Rakshabandhan, prior to this.

Just then the bell rang. The teacher instructed all the students - "All the students should go one by one in a straight line to the gate of the school. Autorikshaw are parked near the main gate in the parking lot".

All the students obeyed the instructions of the class-teacher and moved on slowly to the gate. Shruti and Seema both used to travel from the same autorikshaw and hence, went together.

"You don't tie Rakhi to your brother's hand?" – Seema asked as the auto-rickshaw started from the school.
"No. I don't have a brother." – Shruti replied.

"Ok. It's so sad. I get so many gifts from my brother on Rakhi. I also enjoy a lot of sweets." – Seema said excitedly.
"You get so many gifts? Which sweets do you eat? What all you get? Is it so happy day?" – She asked curiously.

"Yes. I eat kaju-katli, which is my favourite in sweets and everything that I like. It's a very happy day for all the sisters. It is the day of the sisters." – Seema answered happily.

"I asked my brother to gift me a beautiful pink coloured frock, that I saw at the nearby big showroom and he will gift it to me, tomorrow." – Seema added.

Shruti was very excited to know about Rakshabandhan. She was eager to go home and ask her mother about the same. As she entered her house's boundary, she got very curious to ask her mom.
"Why don't we celebrate it? I will tell mom to celebrate it from now." she thought for a while, when she was walking towards the gate of her home.

Her house had a large surface area, though not so big in build-up area yet it was a great place to live near the nature. A collection of plants and trees in the area, which make it to appear green and contributed to the green nature, was like a heaven in itself. Her father, Pramod Singh, an Engineer by occupation was a great nature lover. He liked gardening and that's why he preferred to have a small garden at his home itself.

Her father also had a habit to plant trees on special occasions, like birthdays, etc. He also planted a Neem plant when she was born. He used to take care of his small garden on Sundays and public holidays.

"Ok. So, I will tell mom to celebrate it from now onwards. It will be so exciting to get so many gifts." - She thought as she came near the gate of the house. A cute happiness grew on this 5-year old girl's face as she thought about the gifts.

"Mummy, I have come" – she said delightedly, as she arrived near the wooden gate.
"Come, my little princess. I feel so happy to see you, my princess." – Her mother Indra replied, after opening the gate.

Her mother, Mrs. Indra Singh was an intelligent lady and a caring mother. She was an Engineering graduate but after her birth, turned to house wife to give her the best care. She was also great at cooking and Veg. Pulaao made by her was Shruti's favourite dish.

"Mummy, Will we celebrate Rakhi tomorrow?" – She asked after putting his bag on the chair near the dining table.
Her mother was a bit shocked with her sudden question. She remembered about Rakhi festival celebrations, when she was at her parent's house. She used to have a great time on Rakshabandhan with her three brothers – Rakesh, Mahesh and Shailesh.

But things have changed now. Six long years have been spent without tying Rakhi to anyone. Six years ago, Indra married her love Pramod. They studied at the same college and developed love for each other. When they decided to marry each other, their families were not convinced for the same.

As the marriage was not supported by both the families, Pramod decided to stay separately along with his wife Indra, in his grand-father's old bungalow located in the city itself.

What a lovely day was that, it was a great time as it felt just like a princess. It was a princely feeling as she was the only sisters to three brothers. She thought about the last Rakhi she celebrated with her family, and got nostalgic.

"Mummy, Mummy. Where is my brother? To whom, will I tie my Rakhi?" – Shruti asked, which led her mother to come out of her own thoughts.

She thought for a while & replied, – "Shruti, Why do you need a brother. Don't we love you, princess?"
Shruti replied, "Mom, I have heard that brothers give us gifts, our favourite sweets, and lots more."
"Yes, that is true but we also do provide you with the gifts. Do you want a gift? We will buy you that."– Indra tried to convince her.

"But I want a brother, mom." – She argued.
Her past memories started pictorising in her memory. The day came to her memory, when she met with an accident and as a result her uterus was severely damaged and had to be removed. She was pregnant for the second time, at that time.

It was a big pain for Indra and her husband to bear at that point. But, they bear it and tried their best to forget it.
"Shruti, Go to your room and change your clothes." – Her mother tried to divert the subject of the conversation.
"Mom, I also want a brother. Everybody in my class have their brother, who give them gifts, play with them and give their toys to them. I also want a brother this Rakhi" – she expressed her wish.

"Shruti, go to your room straight away. You can't get a brother." – Indra replied in a strong tone. She knew that this will hurt Shruti, but she herself was quite upset, with this suddenly raised issue.

Shruti was upset on hearing that she will not get her brother. She started weeping and went to her room.

Her mother thought to follow her and to convince her, when someone stopped her from moving forward.

It was Pramod, Indra's husband and the caring father of Shruti. "She can't understand. I can't give her what she wants." – Her mother cried in pain.
Pramod consoled her, "Listen! Don't be sad. She is angry and sad now, I will convince her. Don't worry. Everything will be fine."

"But, her demand is not unusual. I am unable to fulfil her demand. I am feeling guilty for her. I can't fulfil even a small wish she has." – Indra cried helplessly. She loved her daughter and felt her sadness.

"It's not your fault and you know it well. Never say such things. She is an intelligent girl and will understand it. We will convince her for now & explain things later when she will be able to understand it." – He replied.

Pramod along with Indra walked in to her room, where she had got asleep. He rubbed his hands over her head with care and affection.

He then turned towards Indra & whispered, "She is an innocent girl. Like every little girl, she has some dreams, whereas in reality some limitations also exist. We will make her understand and she will understand it."

"But, a male-child is what you wanted and even your family too. Didn't you?" – Indra said as she remembered the day when her mother-in-law called them, when Shruti was born, and ended the phone conversation, when she came to know that it was a baby girl.

"I wanted the second child, but now, that we can't have one, we will try our best to raise Shruti in the best way we can." – Pramod replied.

"Can't we adopt a baby-boy for her. She will be so happy to get her brother." – Indra suggested.

Pramod look towards her and said "Adoption is okay. But, this way it may deprive her of care, she deserves. The little one will need an extra-care and we may not pay attention towards Shruti." – Pramod answered calmly.

Indra replied, "We will give equal attention to both of them. Pramod, please search for some adoption centre."

"What about a test-tube baby?" – Indra added.

"It will cost us a big amount of money. Plus we will have to arrange a surrogate mother too."

"Hmm. That will be a big issue then." – Indra replied as she looked towards Shruti who was sleeping unaware of what her parents were talking about.

2

Shruti got up in the evening and saw her father was reading the newspaper in the living room. She went near to him and sat on the chair.

"How is my little princess?" – Pramod asked
She stood and said, "Papa, I want a brother for this Rakshabandhan."

"Ok. Is it a final decision, my princess?" – said her father in a convincing way. He firmly believed that things can be dealt better with sweet words rather than harsh words.

"Yes Papa. I need a brother this Rakshabandhan. All my friends have brothers whom they tie Rakhi on Rakshabandhan. I also want a brother like them." – She replied.

Pramod thought for a while and said, "So my little princess needs a brother, we will definitely get one for her. Is it okay?"
Her mother's expressions were like she was not agreeing to her father's false commitment regarding the brother. But she was silent as she knew that her husband will handle everything wisely.

On hearing the words of her father, Shruti got very happy.
"Thank you Papa. I love you a lot. You know one thing papa, mom scolded me. She is very bad. She doesn't want that I should meet my brother." – She complained.

Her happiness was indicated by her delighted face. Though, she showed a complaining attitude towards her mother who straight away scolded her for demanding a brother this Rakshabandhan.

"Don't tell this. Your mom loves you a lot and she is the best mom. She takes care of you and me too." – Her father said.
"Hmm, Papa." – She said after thinking. "But, she scolded me. I will not talk with her." – She added.

"No, it's wrong. Say a sorry to her. She is your mom. Don't say like this." – Her father replied.
Her father was her favourite so she had to obey what he said; she stood up & went to the kitchen, where her mother was busy cooking dinner. She went to her and stopped nearby.

"I am sorry mom." She apologized.
"No my princess, I am sorry. You know what I am making for you today?" – Her mother replied.
"Pulaao?" – She asked curiously
"Yes. Pulaao." – Her mother replied.
"Thank you so much, mom" – She said.

She was very excited and came back to her father in a delighted mood. Her father said her, "See how much she loves you."
"Yes."
"Where is my brother?" – She asked her father.

"He will meet you tomorrow, on Rakshabandhan itself. But before meeting him, you will have to hear a story. Will you hear it?" – Her father asked.

"Sure papa, I like stories so much." – She was excited.
"So, here it goes." – Her father started narrating.

"Once upon a time, in a beautiful city lived a cute girl. Her name was Angel. She was so cute that all people admired her cuteness.

Her father and mother were also very proud and happy to have her as their child as she was so intelligent and innocent-looking cute girl.

Her behaviour was very good and her excellent smile added to her cuteness. When she used to wake up from sleep, she didn't cry instead she used to smile, that was a unique feature of her. Her parents were often complimented that their kid will rise up to a great height when she will grow up. These compliments made her mother and father both very proud of her.

One day, the mother and father went to the doctor. The mother was a bit unwell. Doctor conducted a few tests and then told them to wait for some time to collect the reports.
After the time was over, both of them met the doctor who told them that very soon they will be blessed with a baby.

The mother and father were very happy to hear this news. They wanted to share the news with the cute Angel but they thought, they would give her a big surprise later on.
They hide it from her. She was un-aware yet very happy. The family was having a great time till now.

Then one day, a sad thing happened. The mother was cleaning the house, like she did every day. She got imbalanced and fell from the stairs and was very injured. Angel's father rushed her to the hospital.

She was immediately admitted to the hospital and was very serious. The doctor informed the father that the baby who was to come suddenly decided not to come. It was god's decision that the baby will not come.

Additionally the mother's condition too was quite severe and the doctor told the father to pray to the god to save her life. As there were chances that she may also die due to this accident. The father was so sad that he cried in front of the god's idol and prayed to him to save the mother's life. As a result of the prayers by the father, the doctor conducted a small operation as a result of which, the life of the mother was saved.

When she got conscious, she asked about the baby. The doctor informed her about the demise of the baby. She cried a lot hearing about the decision of the god, as both she and her husband had many dreams about the baby. She immediately asked about Angel. Her husband told that Angel is at their neighbour's house.

She was very hopeful to give a big gift to the Angel but she was unable to do so. They hide it from their Angel because they knew that if she will get to know about this, she will also feel very bad.

And they can't see her crying and feeling sad. So, they decided not to tell her till she grows big to be able to understand the things." – Her father narrated. Shruti got sad at the end of the story.

"My princess, now I want to ask a question based on this story to you. Can I?" – Her father asked.
"Yes Papa."

"In the last, the mother and father decided that they will hide it from Angel. Did they do it right?"

Shruti began to think for a while. She replied after thinking, "Yes papa. Their decision was right because they didn't want to make their daughter sad. They loved her so much."
A little smile appeared on the face of her father, as he said,

"Very good, Shruti. Your answer is correct." Her father was glad to know that at this age, she knew emotions and emotional bonding.
"Do you know who the girl Angel is?" – He asked.

Shruti looked at her father curiously and asked, "Who is she? Is this a real story? I want to know about Angel. I want to meet her."
Her father turned to her and said, "That Angel is you, my little daughter."

Shruti was confused with this. She asked, "I am the little angel. Is it true papa?"
"Yes, my princess."

It was a sudden shock to know that the story belong to her. She never thought that her mother and father did hide such a sad thing from her. Tears came in her eyes, as she thought for a while.
"Papa" – she said.
"Yes my princess."

"Why did god do that? And when will god send my brother now?" she asked. "I want to tie a Rakhi on his hand this Rakshabandhan." – She added.

Her mother who was still in tears, listening to the story suddenly outburst her emotions, "Shruti, He will never come now. He will never.." she started crying.

Her father consoled her mother and said - "Please don't cry. We have to live our life. And, we have our princess already. She will make us feel proud."

Shruti came to her mother who was in tears. She tried to swipe her tears & slowly said, "Don't cry mom. I will never ask about my brother now. I will not tie Rakhi. I am sorry mom."

Her mother who was crying till now, consoled her, "No, my princess. Don't be sorry. You have not done anything wrong."
Her father asked suddenly, "Is there someone who will tell me, when the dinner will get ready?" He basically said this to normalize the sad atmosphere prevalent in the house.

Her mother, got up and replied, "It's nearly ready. Let me make the chapattis and bring it. Both of you wash your face till then. No crying now."

Both Shruti and her father were sitting on the chair of the dining table waiting for the dinner. Her mother came up with the chapattis & then her father got up from the chair to help her out. After the things for dinner were arranged, they got seated at their respective places.

Her father initiated the conversation, "Princess, do pass the white container to me. Tell me which dish is in it?"
He did saw it earlier that the dish in white container was Pulaao, but he wanted to see Shruti's reaction.

Shruti got up and saw in the container after lifting the case, she replied casually - "It is pulaao, dad."

Her dad was surprised. Pulaao is her favourite dish of all time and this time she was not excited on seeing Pulaao. It was an indication that she is much sad about the issue.

She also seems like being in her thoughts only which made her father disturbed. Her sadness had replaced her happiness a day before or says some hours before.

Her mother gave her food as per her choice and she took it silently without uttering anything. Everything was very quite at this moment, and one could easily hear the revolving sound of the ceiling fan.

Her father thought for a while and then switched on the TV. Usually when the TV was switched-on and her father switched to a news channel, she would request for a cartoon channel and her request was always accepted normally.

This time no request came from her side. She was eating food without saying anything. She had her whole dinner and then moved to the kitchen to keep her utensils in the washing sink. Then, she silently went to the living room. Her father had finished his dinner by then and came to the kitchen where her mother was washing utensils.

She said him, "She is very sad. I don't know whether we did right or not by telling her about the reality. She was so happy when she came back from the school in the afternoon."

"I know that. But, we didn't have any other option then to reveal the truth to her. She has the right to know this truth."

"But you have promised her that her brother will come tomorrow. What will happen if she asks you about that?" – her mother asked.

Her father thought for a while, and replied calmly, "I have planned regarding this."

"Planned regarding this? Which plan?" – She asked looking at him.

Her husband looked up to her, and replied swiftly, "The plan will be implemented tomorrow. You will have to wait till that time."

He went away from the kitchen after saying this, and his wife (her mother) was left with no option then to wait for the other day.

The day ended with a mixed atmosphere consisting of sadness, emotional distress, curiosity and hope.

3

RAKSHABANDHAN DAY
Her mother rose up early in the morning while Shruti was still asleep.

Her father too got up at the daily time and went to the garden early in the morning. As the day was the scheduled holiday on account of Rakshabandhan the schedule was loosely bound, and not strict.

Her father's usual pattern was that he used to read the newspaper as well as do gardening on Sundays and the public-holidays like this day of Rakshabandhan.

At 8.30am her mother told her to get up. She was sleepy but had to get up as it was her mother's instruction to get up early even during holidays. She got up and went for the daily activities.

By 9.30am, she was having breakfast. Her mother was reading the newspaper when the landline phone rang.
Her mother attended the phone. It was Seema, Shruti's friend on the other side. Her mother handed over the phone to Shruti to talk.

The conversation started:

Seema: Hello, how are you?

Shruti: I am fine. What about you?

Seema: I am also fine. I want to tell you that the auspicious time (Muhurat) for today's Rakshabandhan is from 9.30 to 11.30 in the morning. Do ensure that you do it on time.

Shruti: (turned sad) I will not celebrate it today.

When she said this her mother looked up to her, she however didn't notice it, as she were facing the other side.

Seema: Why? It is the festival of sisters.

Shruti: I am not in mood to celebrate.

Seema: But, why? Is it due to the reason that you don't have any brother?

Shruti: I will call later, bye.

Seema: Ok. As you wish, bye

And she hanged up the conversation. Shruti slowly put down the phone, which indicated that she was still sad.

Her mother also became sad as well as angry when she saw her daughter sad. She was angry over her friend who called her in the very morning to spoil her mood for the whole day.

Seema appeared to her as the biggest villain who tried to steal her happiness of the day.

She remembered that how happy she was when she came from school. She was much excited when her father told her that her brother will come the next day for Rakhi.

As her mother came out of her thoughts, she saw Shruti walking slowly towards the living room. She wanted to stop her but then she thought that she should let her go for now.

"For how much time, she will be sad like this. We need to do something about this" she spoke to herself. Just then she decided something and thought she should go and talk with her husband about it.

With such thoughts in mind, she walked to the entrance gate of the house which landed her in the parking lane. She had to cross this lane to reach the garden, where her husband Pramod was.

The big bungalow in which the family lived was among the few preserved green places in the city. With the expansion of city and the modernisation, the green belt of the city had decreased by a greater percentage.

"Pramod, where are you?" – She called out loudly. But she could not find him in the back garden as she saw across the garden.

It was strange as he usually spends much time in the backside garden as it had huge grass which needs to be trimmed periodically with the grass trimmer. She could not see the grass trimmer anywhere nearby so she concluded that he was not there.

She was thinking about this when she caught view of the main gate of the house. Pramod was standing near the gate talking with someone on the phone facing the gate.

She reached to him and instead of interrupting in between the conversation, simply went in front of him. She looked sad, which Pramod anticipated and hinted that he will end the conversation soon.

For Shruti's mother, waiting for a minute too was a big deal as she was much concerned about her daughter. Anyways, she kept waiting for five minutes, and then the conversation came to an end. Pramod ended the conversation and with this, she lost her patience.

"Can you tell me that do you care for your daughter?" she asked.
"She is very sad and at this time too, you are busy with the phone conversation instead of devising ways to make her happy." she added.

She was very sad and angry at the way Pramod was dealing with the issue.
Pramod was shocked with her reaction. In many years of a successful married life, she never spoke to her in such a high tone then she was speaking today.

"Cool down, Indra." He tried to convince her. "She is my daughter too and I am also equally concerned about her. Do you know whom I was talking to?" he asked.

Seeing her silent, Pramod replied, "I was talking to my Advocate friend Mayank, who was also my classmate and a close-friend. I was requesting him to come to her house so that Shruti can tie Rakhi to his son Tarun."

"What did he say? Is he coming?" – She asked instantly.
"He told me that he will come as soon as his wife returns from her brother's house." – said Pramod.
This was a comforting statement for Indra. She was concerned for her daughter and this brought a sigh of relief on her face.

Just then, she realized her mistake. She realized that she would not have spoken to her husband in such a harsh and angry voice.

She said "I am sorry" and broke down to tears.

Pramod came close to her and said, "I know you love Shruti a lot. You are her mother. But don't forget I am also concerned about her as she is my daughter too."

She hugged and tears began to flow still. Pramod wiped her tears and said, "Don't shred your tears this way. It's a happy moment for our daughter."

She smiled and hugged him again. This time, he too hugged her and said, "Let me tell you something. Till I am alive, don't feel insecure, neither you nor our daughter. Mind it."
She agreed to his saying and both stayed there for a while.

When they were about to go back to the house, she asked, "How old is Tarun?"
Her husband, looked at her and replied, "He is 1 year elder to Shruti."
"Ok. What are his favourite sweets?" – She enquired. She wanted to bring something that would make him too happy.
"I don't know exactly. But I think he will like the famous Rasgulla and that too from the famous shop located in Wings Road area." – He replied.

"I think I should also take her along to the market, to buy Rakhi and Sweets." – She said happily.

As she walked to the entrance of the house, she was very excited. The excitement was to see the happiness on Shruti's face, on hearing that her brother will come on this Rakshabandhan.

She directly went to Shruti's room, where she observed that Shruti was sitting lonely.

She came near to Shruti and sat down on the bed. Shruti saw her mother but didn't spoke anything.

"Shruti, How are you my princess?" – Her mother asked.

"I am fine mom. I am not sad, don't worry about me." – She replied slowly.

Her mother anticipated and realized that she was just pretending but in reality, she was sad she spoke to her, "Get ready. We are going out to the market."

Shruti turned to her mother, and asked "Market? Why for?"

4

"It's for the first time that my princess will tie Rakhi on wrist of her brother. So, we should go and buy Rakhi for her brother definitely. Isn't it?" – Her mother said.

She turned happy on hearing this. It was what she wanted the most. She asked – "Mom, is it true? My brother is coming? Will he come on this Rakshabandhan? God has sent him?" she asked.

Now her father Pramod had also arrived to the room. He was so happy to see the mother-daughter happy and peacefully.
Seeing him, she got happy and said, "Papa, I love you. You are very nice. Thank you so much papa."

He put his hand on her head and said, "Papa love you too, my princess. Always have this smile on your face."
She turned back to her mother and said excitedly, "Mom, I will take the best Rakhi for my brother."

Just then she asked curiously, "What is his name?"
Her mother was happy to see her delighted and was about to reply her, but just then her father interrupted in between -

"That's a surprise for my little princess."
"Please let me know at least the first alphabet of his name. I want to buy a keychain that I saw at JBS Shopee. I want to buy it for him." – She requested.

Her father smiled on hearing this. He was very happy to see her happy. Her curiosity too made him happy for the fact that how much she wants her brother in her life.

He replied, "Ok. If that's it then the first alphabet is T"
"Wow, that's so sweet papa. What is the full name papa? Please tell me" – she asked again.

Her father said in a complaining way, "Now this is cheating. You asked for the first alphabet and now you are asking the full name. It doesn't work this way."

Just then, her mother said, "Shruti, go and get ready. We will have to leave the house early so that we can get the things ready before your brother comes."

"Yes mom." – She said excitedly and went to the room for getting ready fast. Her mother too went with her so as to help her with her selection of clothes. Though, she was quite choosy about the clothes but still her mother's choice dominated the decision mostly.

Her father was very happy standing at his position for now too. He was thinking, how good it were if they could fulfil her wish of a brother themselves. But that was not in their hands. The doctor told them that if they want to fulfil their wish, they would have to opt for surrogacy which is a quite expensive procedure.

Then her father affirmed her decision to make Tarun, her 'Rakhi brother'. He was happy as how easily Mayank agreed to his request.

"I think I should get a gift for Mayank too. He is a really nice friend of mine and so deserves a gift." – Her father spoke to himself.

Her father was in his own thoughts, when a voice diverted his attention, "Papa, I am ready."
He turned to see her. She was looking just like an angel in the light-pink coloured dress. This dress was the same which her mother brought for her birthday.

"Come, my little princess. You are looking so cute, my princess." – Her father complimented.
She got delighted on listening this and then she realized that she forgot something.
"Papa, I forgot my hair band. I must bring it." She said & rushed to the living room for this.

Her father looked towards the entrance of the living room to see her running swiftly to the room. Her way of walking calmed him of the fact that she is very happy and excited. It made him to smile.

Just then he experienced a hand on his arm. It was his better-half. He turned to her and smiled to which she reciprocated.
"Pramod, It feels so nice to see her happy. Isn't it?" she asked slowly.
"Yes. May god give her lots of happiness always! It feels like heaven to see her happy" – he replied.

She smiled and asked, "Have you enquired when they are coming? I mean the time, so that everything is done in the auspicious time (muhurat)."

"Mayank will call me once his son Tarun and his wife reach the house. I don't know about the auspicious time for Rakhi, though." – He said.

"Ok. I need to inquire about the auspicious time of the Rakhi from one of my friends. I am untouched from it for nearly 6 years as of now." – Her mother replied sadly.
"I know that. No problem. I will ask Mayank about it. Till you go to the market and get the required things." – He said.

Just then Shruti came back from the room. She was living very cute with the shining red coloured hair band which she wore. It was her favourite and she looked very nice wearing it.

"Bye papa." – She said while she was leaving for the market to buy things, most importantly the Rakhi for her brother. She was overly excited for the same.

After closing the gate, he heard the phone vibration sound. He went but till that time the vibration sound stopped. The phone's display light was on which indicated that someone called. Her father took the phone and saw it was Mayank's contact no.s.

"Ok. A call from Mayank! I should call him back to ask when he is coming?" – he murmured.
"Oh! A busy tone" – her father whispered before he hanged up the call.

This made him feel strange.
"Why did he cut the phone?" he wondered.
He tried again but still in vain. Just after 2-3 rings he got the busy tone again. He stopped for a while, thinking that may be Mayank might be trying to call him, but no call back from his side.

He called him again after 10 minutes, this time on the landline phone.

The domestic maid picked up the phone. He asked about Mayank to which he replied:
"Sir, Sahab is not there at the moment. He has left a message for you. He wants to meet you here, at the house in half an hour."

"Is this message for Pramod Singh?" – He tried to re-confirm.
"Yes sir. Do come over here in half an hour. Sahab will directly reach the house then." – He replied.

He ended the conversation. He was unable to understand the whole thing. If he is busy how can he be at home in half an hour? Why he called him before but not answering now? Many questions like these arose in his mind.

"He might be busy. I should call Indra to inform her that I will go there to visit him and then we will come together I suppose that's what he has planned"– He decided.

He called Indra and told her about the whole incident. Indra asked him about the reason of calling him to home first. He replied to her that he himself was confused over the sudden change of venue, as previously Mayank was to visit their place.

He reached there, exactly after half- an hour. It was 15 minutes drive from his house and as he knew it from he knew the landmark and the proper location.

Mayank's house was a big bungalow surrounded by greenery in the front. He was from a well to do family and his father was a well-known lawyer of the city. Pramod remembered as to how much, he was impressed with the big library in his house which was stocked with plenty of books.

AT THE DRAWING ROOM

"Sir has told that you should get seated. He will be there any time soon." – The domestic maid announced.
Pramod looked up to him. He was an 18-something tall boy with a strong physique; probably from a rural background.

"Ok. What is your name by the way?" – Pramod asked as he took the glass of water in hand from the table.
Domestic maid replied slowly, "Raju"
"From where do you belong to?" – Pramod asked.
"I belong to a nearby village 60km away from this place." – Raju replied.

"Ok." – Pramod said as he kept viewing the drawing room, which was a big hall consisting of expensive designer items to give it an attractive look.

Just then the sound of car attracted his attention. It was Mayank's SUV which had arrived finally.

Raju rushed to the gate saying, "Sir, Saheb has arrived."
Pramod thought to go to the gate to meet Mayank, and he stood up. He was about to go when the phone rang. It was his wife's call. He started talking to her.

5

She was asking about the time when they will reach home for
Rakhi, to which he said, "He has just arrived at home along with
his family.

I will talk for a while and will inform you when we will leave for
home."
"I will call you back later." – he replied and ended up the
conversation, as he saw Mayank coming from the gate.

Mayank, his friend had an amazing dressing sense. While in
school and college days too he dressed so well in a professional
manner. Now, being an LLB from the best college of India and
LLM from a prestigious college in London, his personality got
more superb with the qualifications he acquired.

"Hey Pramod! How are you?" – He asked Pramod.
Pramod was happy to see his all time best friend Mayank.
Though they had not met for quite some time after he did his
Law course, still he was a very nice friend.

"I am fine Mayank. What about you?" – He replied.
Mayank and Pramod shook hands and got seated on the sofa
lying in the hall. Just then a cute boy arrived in a playful happy
mood. He was Tarun.

As he arrived near Mayank, he said him, "Tarun, look he is
Pramod uncle."
Tarun greeted him by joining his hands in the form as to say

him Namaste to which he replied happily. Just then Mayank's wife came. She looked a bit unhappy.

On seeing her, Mayank said to Pramod, "Meet my wife Anjali." Pramod got up from the sofa and greeted her, "Namaste Bhabhiji."

"Namaste" – She greeted her back. It looked like she was not much happy to see him and greeted in a formal way.

After some formal interaction, she went to the inside of house from the drawing hall. Tarun also went with his mom to the inside of the house.

Mayank and Pramod were interacting about their college days and everything they did and enjoyed. Both got nostalgic about the school days.

Just then Pramod said him, "I am very thankful to you for agreeing to let Shruti tie Rakhi on hand of Tarun. It will be very nice. She is very happy about it and waiting for her brother."

Mayank looked at Pramod. He started smiling and replied after a while, "No need to thank me. It's alright."

Pramod replied in an emotional manner, "No it is a big thing for me. After the demand of Shruti the earlier day, we were confused what to do? When you called me the first thing that I had in mind was this. I can't see her in pain. I am very much grateful of you." Pramod was about to cry.

Mayank interrupted and said, "Control yourself Pramod, Friends are meant to help each other. Never think this. If Shruti is getting a brother with this, Tarun is also getting a little sister.

Both of them are being benefited."

They both were quite happy. Pramod was very happy that in spite of being a well known lawyer with a high status, Mayank was still down to earth. They both were sipping coffee and enjoying a healthy conversation when Raju came.

"Sir, Ma'am has sent me to tell you that she is calling you for an important work"
"Ok. Tell her I am coming" – Mayank said

As Raju went away, Mayank turned to Pramod and said, "I am going inside to talk to Anjali regarding this, and I am sure she will also agree to it. Then we will accompany you to your home. I am sure you are not getting late."
"No problem. I am fine." – Pramod said.

Pramod saw as Mayank went to the room inside. He was very happy that now finally his daughter, his princess will be getting her brother, her most liked gift.

Just as a matter to spend the time in between, he glance a look at the table which was containing several newspapers and other periodicals arranged in a very neatly manner.

He took the latest edition of the automobile magazine and started reading it. The first page of it were relating to the same car which he was planning to buy for a long time.

He was reading to it word by word, when he heard a female loud voice. The voice interrupted him from reading and he glanced towards the direction from where voice was coming. The voice was coming from the room where Mayank went. He assumed it was Anjali, the wife of Mayank.

The voice was clear but in a very low tone. He tried not to hear and appear as if he was not hearing any voice. Just then he realised what Mayank said, he will be talking about the Rakhi matter with his wife. This made him alert.

"I should see, what is the matter?" – He thought for a while and got up from the sofa.
Just then another thought arose in his mind, "Is it fine to listen to their conversation? It's their private issue and he should not intervene in it."

He moved towards the outer room, whose gate was closed. As he went near to the gate the voice became clear. Anjali was talking in a loud voice with Mayank.
"I don't want to listen anything. My decision is final" – said Anjali in a loud/angry tone.
"But I have promised to him and he is waiting for us." – Mayank said in a comparative low tone.

"You don't know such people. I know them well" – Anjali replied

Mayank interrupted her and said, "I know him since childhood. He is not like this."
"You are sincere. You don't know the intentions of these people."

"What are you trying to say? Don't just talk nonsense."
"This Rakhi thing is just an excuse. The main thing, he wants is valuable gifts for his daughter from us every year. He wants a rich brother for his daughter." – Anjali replied.

After hearing Anjali's reply, Pramod was shocked. He was feeling like he will faint any moment. The door was still closed. He never thought in this way. He was feeling so sad to hear how his childhood friend Mayank's wife Anjali misunderstood about his intentions regarding the pure and auspicious occasion of Rakhi.

He silently went away from the door and came near the sofa, where he was sitting a couple of minutes before. After hearing this he decided not to stay there anymore.
He just went out of the house without saying anything.
The moment he sat in his car, he was feeling so sad and angry.

"How can they think that about me? I am myself a self made professional and I and my daughter don't need their valuable gifts. What they think of mine?" – He thought to himself.

He looked at the big bungalow with anger and then his hand moved to the key to switch on the car. As he was about to start the car, his phone rang. Indra was calling to him.

He could figure out that what she was calling to ask. She must be asking about the time when they will come to the house. He ignored her call and started the engine of the car. The car moved toward the destination. He was disinterested to go to home, but he was concerned about his wife and daughter. They will be much concerned about him and what if they call to ask Mayank about his whereabouts.

He reached home, and parked his car outside the house.
He locked the car and came to the greenery of the outer garden.

He was feeling like he should cry any moment. He can't even

fulfil a single small wish of his daughter. This thought made him much sad. He was thinking that how will he face his daughter now, who might be waiting for the arrival of her brother.

Just then the voice of Anjali rose in her voice, as she was saying, "He wants a rich brother for his daughter" "He wants a rich brother for his daughter" "He wants a rich brother for his daughter".

This thing happened multiple times and he was about to scream a loud "No". Just then he noticed a soft hand over his collar. It was Indra. She was waiting for him and she came to know that he has arrived.

"What happened, Pramod? Where are they?" – she asked sadly. Pramod turned towards her, and replied, "They will not come. They won't let my princess tie Rakhi to their son's wrist." Indra listened to it and asked, "What happened? Tell me."

Pramod looked up to her eyes and then turned his eyes down. He narrated the whole story to Indra. She listened to it calmly and then paused for a while.

They were standing near the fencing of the front-garden of their house. Pramod was confused and was looking out for a solution to this.

He stopped just before the fencing and stood there for a while. His wife was not able to understand what was going on. She understood that he is very sad and tried to console him, "Please don't get upset. We should forget this and I will talk with some friend of mine."

"No. I don't want my daughter to beg in front of anyone for a brother now." – Pramod said in a bold voice. Indra was shocked to listen it as she thought he will get hopeful for the same.

"My little princess needs not to tie her precious Rakhi on any random guy now. I have chosen a brother for her. And, I hope she will like it." – He replied confidently which indicated he had found a solution for the problem.
"Who" – Indra asked curiously.

"Here, he is." – Pramod said, as he pointed out to the Neem plant, planted alongside the fence.
"Who? Are you talking about this plant?" – Indra asked.

"Yes. If you remember this, we both planted this plant alongside the fence when we came to this house and you were about to be admitted to the hospital for the delivery of the baby .i.e. our little princess. I planted the sapling and you watered it for the first time." – He said.

6

Indra replied, "Yes. I remember. This way it is older then Shruti, some days only though."

A ray of hope arose on the face of Pramod as he heard Indra's views. It meant that he got the answer to everything.

"Our daughter will make this plant as her brother and tie Rakhi to it. It will secure us and hear. It will be a confidence for her always." – He said confidently.

"But, what about the people's view on this? They will make fun of her. A plant as a brother, it may sound as weird thing" – Indra replied.

To this, Pramod replied confidently, "I don't care about the people. It will impart confidence to my daughter. We both are nature lovers. And, as we know all natural things breathe and live life. And as per the taxonomic classification all the species of the nature are inter-related to each other."

Indra who was not agreeing to him, now agreed. It was known to her that both of them were nature lovers and that's why they used to plant saplings on special occasion, whether it be the local colony ground in their home district that was converted into a garden or it be the free land situated behind their college that was converted with their efforts to a big garden which now consisted of big trees that give shade to various people.

Indra said, "If it's your final decision, then it's ok. But, I doubt that Shruti will agree to it. She may get confused or sad to hear this." She agreed to him but she was also uncertain about the reaction of Shruti when she will come to know that they have decided to make a tree as her brother.

Both of them went to their home and decided to tell everything to their princess. She was unaware of their decision and was sitting watching her favourite program on the television in the living room.

As they entered the room, Shruti got excited and said, "Mummy Papa, Have you brought my brother with you? Where is he?" and she looked here and there.

She was about to go to the drawing room/hall in search of him when Pramod stopped her and said, "Yes my princess. We have brought him. But, firstly you get ready with the Rakhi first. Then we will go and meet him."

Shruti got excited. "Yes dad, I am completely ready."
"Ok. Where is the Rakhi & other items which will be required? You will also do tilak and for it you will require kumkum." – her father replied.

Shruti paused for a while and then went out fastly to the drawing room/hall.
"I hope she will like what we have thought for her?" – Indra asked hopefully.
"She will like it. She is our daughter, our princess & she will obey our decision full mindedly." – Pramod replied confidently.

Just then Shruti came to the room with the plate in which everything were neatly arranged ranging from the Rakhi to the kumkum, rice, etc. Her mother had arranged the contents of this plate and kept it in the kitchen.

"Here it is. Now please take me to my brother. I am excited to meet my brother." – She said excitedly.

Indra and Pramod both were hopeful but yet sort of uncertain about the reaction of Shruti when she will meet her 'brother'. They were mentally make up about the situation and were ready to face the situation.

"That's good, my princess. So lets go." – Her father said.
"Yeah." – Shruti said excitedly.
They all went to the entrance of the house. With every step they were taking, they were somewhat thinking about the possible outcome.

Her mother looked toward her father, who too reciprocated. He was confident and hinted her to be confident herself too.
An understanding couple is the best. When one of them is emotionally down or confused, the other one tries their best to uplift their confidence and the things are easily manageable.

They both saw Shruti whose eyes were searching all around for her brother but were not able to find him. Finally, all three of them reached the gate of the garden .i.e. the main gate of their house.

As they stopped, Shruti asked impatiently - "Papa, where is my brother? I can't see him anywhere around?"
Her mother and father both were silent on this but then, her father replied, "Here, he it is. It's the Neem." – as he pointed out his finger to the Neem plant that was planted just close to the entrance of the garden.

"Neem? It's a tree, dad." – Shruti asked confusingly.
Her father got near to her, looked at her and said, "Yes, my

princess. You understood right. It's the tree that is your brother from now onwards."

Shruti thought for a while and replied, "But dads, Brothers give sweets to their sisters, talk with them, play with them and also protect them. How will a tree do all this?"

Her father smiled and replied, "See my princess; you can play with your brother, Neem. It protects from diseases. They are great benefits from your brother."

Shruti replied, "But, what about sweets? All my friends were talking that their brothers accompany them to school. Even Sujata's little brother studies in Nursery in the same school." Pramod looked towards Indra, whose uncertainity increased when Shruti started asking her queries. She concluded that Shruti will not agree to them from the queries she was asking.

Pramod looked to Shruti and replied, "Listen, you know one thing, my princess. You are so special compared to all your classmates. And, so is your brother. He may not accompany you to school, or may not talk with you. But, he will always be there to protect you and everyone around."

He added, "And regarding the sweets, that your mother and I will bring it on behalf of your brother. Isn't it fine?"
"It is very nice. I love Rasgulla. But.." Shruti said.
Her father interrupted her in-between and said, "No but, now as the muhurat is going, tie the Rakhi in the auspicious time limit to your brother. TIE the Rakhi and then in the evening we will go out for a dinner at Food Plaza, my princess."

Shruti got happy and said, "Yes papa, I will tie the Rakhi. Mom, please unpack the Rakhi and give it to me."

Her mother, who was uncertain about the reaction of Shruti, now got satisfied to see the way how her husband convinced her lovely daughter.

Both the husband-wife was very happy to see their lovely daughter happy.

Her mother handed her the Rakhi, she took it in hand and then moved closer to the tree and stopped after coming close to the tree. She thought for a while which made her parents especially her mother, a bit tensed. After a while she moved around and asked her father innocently - "Where to tie the Rakhi?"

Her father understood her confusion and took a glance at the tree. He then lifted her up to the height of a interlocking of the small branches and said, "Here it is. Tie the Rakhi."

She was about to tie the Rakhi when her mother said, "Wait!" as she raised the plate in front of Shruti.

"First do a tilak of your brother." – She added. She helped her to do the tilak of her brother and then it was the time for the Rakhi.

She tied the Rakhi on the interlocking of the branches of the tree. Her father helped her to tie the knot. She did it and then her mother and father started clapping.

Just then his father realized something. He searched his pocket and picked out the mobile phone and gave it to her mother for capturing the photo of the same.

Her mother took the same and saw that there was a missed call from Mayank. She got upset to view it and said, "A missed call from Mayank ji?"

Pramod was standing near to her so he heard it and replied nearly instantly, "Ignore it. Capture me with my princess and her brother"

"Smile please!" – Her mother said as she was about to capture the photo. Just then Shruti put an arm over the branch to which she tied Rakhi a couple of minutes ago.

Her mother who was capturing the photo realized it and it made her happy. She was very happy as it was directly from her heart that she offered a care to the Neem tree, without being said to do so.

"Clicked" – she said as soon as she captured the picture.
Her father bent down as Shruti hinted him that she wants to get down. Her father went to her mother in an excitement to see how the photo was.

7

He was also amazed to see the smile on face of his wife as she showed it to him.

"See this." – his wife showed him, how their daughter raised her arm affectionately towards the tree.

This made the couple very happy. They were very happy to know that their daughter has started to care about the Neem tree, her brother.

"Papa.." – Shruti said.

Her father turned around to see that she posed along with the tree. She was looking happy. "Please take one picture of just me and my brother" – she said.

"Off course, my princess" – his father said and focussed the camera towards her and clicked the photo.

"Thank you so much papa." – Shruti was very happy that her father fulfilled her wish.

She was enjoying a lot with her 'brother' as she was having a great time.

AFTER TIEING THE RAKHI

The family of three came to the house for lunch. It was 4pm and the lunch time was 1.5-2 hours late then the usual time.

But all of them were happy at the moment. Shruti was happy that finally she got her brother, her father and mother were happy to see their princess happy.

At the dining table, Shruti and her mother – father were having lunch. Just then she spoke, "Mummy, I will tell everybody in my class that now I also have a brother."

Her mother and father looked towards each other and then her father asked, "Did someone say something to you, my princess?"
Shruti looked at her father and replied innocently, "Yes papa, everyone was asking about my plan for Rakhi. I told them that I had no idea about Rakhi and I will ask my mom."

Her father, stood up and came near to her and said, "My princess, now that you know everything about Rakhi, it will be easy for you to answer them, Right?"

"Right Papa." She replied confidently.
"Now, I will say them that my brother is very special. He is always there to protect me and my family at our house" – she added.

"Shruti, but I think.....%" her mother tried to tell but was stopped by her father
"Yes my intelligent daughter" – her father replied supporting her views as he wondered how easily she accepted the tree as her brother.

But, her mother was still not agreeing to it. She was silent but her way indicated that she was not agreeing to the conversation. Her father observed this but was thinking for an opportunity to talk with her to clarify things.

"Papa, I am going to watch my favourite cartoon. I have finished my lunch." – she said as she showed empty plate to her father. It was a mandatory thing to do as per her mother's saying. She used to eat half and waste half and due to this it caused wastage of food.

Her mother knew this and so she mandated that whenever she will finish food she will show the empty plate to either her father or her mother and then put it for washing.

"Ok my princess." – Her father replied calmly.
As she went her father asked her mother, "What happened?"
Her mother looked toward him and replied, "I will tell her not to tell anything about her brother to anyone in school."

"What's the reason?"
"You don't know. Children at school will make fun of her for this. No one has done this before. They will tell her that she is crazy." – She raised the possibilities.

"No one will tell anything. And for your convenience if any such thing happens, we will ask her tomorrow and handle the situation, if needed." – He tried to convince.

"But, she is a kid and.." – She replied but was interrupted.
"You know one thing. When she accepted her brother, she was convinced by heart about it. We will talk with her. We want to make her strong, won't we?"

"Yes, but this way. She is too young to face these things. She may get depressed with people all around making fun of her." – Her mother replied.
"We will not let it happen. But, if we safeguard her this way, what will happen later when we will not be there?" – Her father said.

"Hmm.. I think that is true. But, I am still worried about her." –

Her mother said.

"Even I also care about her. But, if her choice to comply with our decision is permanent, she may face such situations anytime in life. And, she needs to know how to handle these things."

Her mother paused for a while. She replied, "Yes. I also hope everything will go right for her. I can't see her depressed in any case."

"We will never let such position arise. Have faith in me." – her father assured.

"I have complete faith in you, Pramod " – She said.
"Thank you! That is what I want." – He replied happily.

AFTER DINNER

Shruti slept early after the dinner and watching her favourite cartoon channel for a while because she had to go to school the next day. Her father didn't ask for the news channel as he was happy to see her happy. Before sleeping, it was Pramod's daily routine to talk for a while with her better half Indra.

He enjoyed a cup of tea before going to the bed.
As he sipped the tea, Indra asked her, "Did he called you after that?"

"Who?" Pramod asked
"Mayank ji. I thought maybe he called you after that time." – she replied

Pramod replied, "No, after that I turned off my phone. And frankly speaking, now I don't want to talk to him. He is my

childhood friend, how can he think that for me or my daughter?"
He got sad for a while. He remembered how happy he was when he met Mayank after a long time. They were 'best friends' at school.

Indra said him, "Forget it. Don't be sad. I can't see you sad."
"These words are very precious for me." – Pramod said as he kept the cup back on the table after he drank the tea.
"And, you are very precious for me." – Indra replied calmly hand in hand, which made both of them smile for a while.

NEXT DAY

Shruti got up for her school. This morning she was quite excited to go to school as she was overly excited to share the news about her brother with all her friends.

She got up on first reminder by her mother which made her mother surprised. Her father was reading the newspaper early in the morning, when her mother said him, "Look! She is very excited to go to school today."

Her father looked at her sipping his tea from the cup and observed that she was very happy and then replied, "Yes! She is my princess. And I wish she should be happy always."

"I too wish the same, Pramod." – Her mother said in a calm way. She was confident after the discussion that in any case they will handle everything and nothing bad will happen.

"Indra, tell her to get ready. I will be ready in 5 minutes and will drop her to school and then go directly to the office." – Her father said.

Her mother got surprised with this, she asked, "You will drop her to school today. Why?"

"Her taxi driver called me two days back that he will not come today. I told you about this" – her father reminded her.

"Oh. I am sorry. I am forgetting things these days." – Her mother complained.

"You have to remember so many things and you get stressed too. This is the reason of this. Keep calm." – Her father replied.

"Why I need to fear, when you are here for me and my daughter." – Her mother replied calmly.

"I am ready Papa." – Shruti came and surprised both of them. They were surprised because at usual days at this time, she rushes to get ready but today she was fully ready.

She said this and moved outside the wooden gate. Her mother and father were very happy to see a good change in her.

They always wanted to see her happy and delighted and this had happened. They went outside to the entrance of the house.

Shruti was standing near to the tree. It seemed like she was saying something to the tree. Due to the distance, they were unable to hear but they were very happy to see that she calmly hugged the tree and then turned back to return to the house where she saw both her mother and father with a smile on their face.

"What were you doing Shruti" – Her mother asked with a smile.

"Mummy, I thanked my brother for coming to me for Rakhi. And I hugged him and told him to stay with us always. He will fulfil my wish, mummy?" she asked

"Yes off course, he will fulfil because he is your brother and you are her sister." – her mother answered.

Her father smiled when he heard a positive answer from her mother. Finally she was convinced. Usually when new things are inducted, it takes some time to get normal.

"I am getting late for the school. We should go now." – Shruti said.

"Yes my princess. We are departing right now. We just realized today that you like your school so much." – Her father joked

She got delighted and happy as she thought it's a praise.

AT THE SCHOOL

When she reached the school, she was overly excited to meet her friends, especially those who were bragging about their brother, etc on the day before Rakhi.

She met Seema in the class room and asked, "How are you? How was your Rakhi?"

Seema replied instantly, "I had so much fun this Rakhi. I enjoyed playing for the whole day with my cousins, and also my own brother."

On being asked about hers, Shruti replied proudly, "I also had a great fun with my brother. I played around him whole day. We captured so many pictures with him. I also tied Rakhi to him and enjoyed the day."

Seema was confused over this and asked right away, "Your brother? Where is your brother? Is he your cousin?"

To this, Shruti said, "He is my real special brother. I love him a lot. I enjoy playing around him. He is always there at my house to protect me."

8

Seema got confused with this. She went with her mother to Shruti's house twice earlier and she knew that she did not have a brother. As she was asking her, 3-4 classmates also arrived in the class room.

She asked, "Your brother is at your home? When he came?"
"He is there since my birth. My mother and father planted him. He is so nice. Give me shade." – She replied proudly
"What does 'planted' means? Who is your brother?" – Mohit asked.

"It's the green tree that is planted near the main gate of my house. It's my brother" – Shruti replied proudly.
All the classmates paused for a while and then Mohit chuckled. "How can a tree be anybody's brother? So you have a brown coloured brother?"

"Tree is your brother. Then how can he play with you? Are you mad?" – Seema asked in a way so as to tease her.
"If tree is your brother then bring your brother to school tomorrow. We want to meet him. Hahaha!" – Rahul said and broke to laughter. Shruti was speechless on these comments.

She thought it would make her feel proud but they all were madly laughing at her. Just then the teacher came to the class room.
"Silent! Silent! All the students maintain pin drop silence." – The teacher ordered.

"Yes madam" – All the students replied in a single voice
Teacher came near to Rahul bench and asked, "Rahul, Getup from the bench and tell me why were you laughing so loudly?"
Rahul got up seriously and replied, "Nothing ma'am"
Teacher asked him again, "Either tell me correctly or get out of the class."

Rahul paused for a while and then looked at Shruti and Mohit and then replied, "Madam, Shruti is saying to everyone that she has a tree brother."

Teacher took a glance at him angrily and turned towards Shruti and asked her, "Shruti! Is he telling right?"
Shruti was hesitating to speak in front of the teacher. She gathered courage on repeated asking and replied, "Yes ma'am, I have a special brother tree. I tied Rakhi to it yesterday on occasion of Rakshabandhan."

Teacher was shocked to learn about it. She never heard such story from anyone in the class. She observed that on listening to this, other students too started whispering in low tone with each other in the class.

She announced, "I want pin drop silence in this class. Is it clear?" And the whole class became silent with her voice. She turned to Shruti and said, "Follow me to the Principal ma'am."
"Ma'am, but I am not telling a lie. Please ma'am" – she requested, but the teacher did not pay attention to her and moved on with her to the principal's office.

The Principal was on round and was standing near the way to the front corridor when in between the teacher met her along with Shruti.

The Principal Malti Sinha was a very descent lady and had the experience of handling big strength schools. After hearing to the teacher, she paused for a while. She then turned to Shruti and asked her peacefully, "Don't be afraid of anyone. Speak the truth. Is it true that you have a tree brother? Who told you about this?"

It was the first instance for Shruti to speak with the Principal. She was a very innocent girl and no complaint was ever filed against her by any classmate. She was afraid and started crying.

She said, "Ma'am, please don't give me TC. I have not done anything". She sobbed.

Principal replied, "No one will give you TC, Shruti. But tell me who told you about the tree brother?"

Shruti stopped for a while and then narrated the whole story as to how she got her brother tree. The Principal was a well experienced person and after a short span of thinking, she sent her back to the classroom and assured her that her name will not be struck off from the school, due to this.

The Principal called her father immediately to the school. She did not however disclose the reason of calling them. Pramod and Indra both were quite anxious to know what happened and reached the school as early as possible.

PRINCIPAL'S OFFICE

"I am Pramod Singh, father of Shruti. She is her mother. We want to know about the reason for being called to the school so urgently?" – Her father asked anxiously.

Principal took a look at them as she was signing a teacher's leave application. As the peon left with the application, she looked towards her father and said, "Sir, we have immediately called you because we wanted to discuss something that was of utmost importance at this moment."

"Are her grades bad? Has she not done her homework? Please illustrate madam to make it clear" – her father asked.
The Principal rang the office bell and called the peon.
"Call Shruti Singh from Class-I" – the Principal ordered the peon who was sitting outside the chamber.

"Ok madam." – He replied and went to execute her order.
"Madam, please tell us that what is her fault that you have called us to the office so urgently." – Her father asked worriedly.

Her mother was constantly looking at her father and the Principal. The Principal saw them anxiously standing and waiting and then said, "Please calm down and be seated."

Both of them got seated but their worries still persisted. The Principal looked again at the file which she was studying for a while and saw outside from the window. Both of them were thinking about the possible reasons.

Seeing both of them tensed, the Principal asked her father, "Mr. Singh, Is it right that Shruti has tied Rakhi to a tree, this Rakshabandhan?"

The question made her mother nervous. She anticipated this outcome previously also, but her father convinced her and now things have worsen to the extent that, both of them were called to the school.

Her father replied, "Yes. I told Shruti to do so."
Just then the peon arrived with Shruti. Shruti was very nervous on seeing her both parents sitting in front of the Principal. She remembered the last time such instance happened a year ago when she was in Prep, when Tushar's parents were seated before the Principal and the next day they were informed that Tushar has been given TC.

"So Shruti, your father told you to tie the Rakhi to the tree?" – Principal asked
"Yes madam." – She replied slowly.

Shruti thought that the same may happen to her too as a result, she started crying. Her mother tried to stop her from crying.

Just then the Peon again came and the principal ordered him
"Tell all the class teachers to take students to the Seminar room. I need to make an important announcement."
"Ok madam."

The peon went but the order by the Principal confused her father and mother about what is going to be happening next. Her father also got worried when he heard that the Principal will be making an important announcement.

He was about to say something, when the Principal interrupted, "Mr. And Mrs. Singh, please come along with me to the Seminar room. I will make an announcement, in which your presence is essential."

AT THE SEMINAR ROOM

All the students and the teachers of the school gathered at the Seminar room. All were discussing about the reason of an emergency announcement.

When the Class-1st arrived they saw that Shruti was sad and was standing with her father and mother on the front stage of the Seminar room just near to the place where the Principal stands when delivery speeches.

"I think Shruti will be given TC today. Look, her mummy-papa has also arrived" – Rahul whispered to Mohit.

"Rahul, I have heard that when one is given TC, they never get admission in any school" – Mohit replied.

Shruti and her parents were struck and confused as to what will be happening in sometimes from now. Her parents were confused and various thoughts came in their mind and the students too were curious to know as of why, they were called to the Seminar room at a short span notice. The whispering still continued even after the Principal reached on the stage.

"Listen Students, I want a pin drop silence in the room." – instructed the Principal.

All the students were silent as of now. Principal was known to be a very strict person due to which even the higher classes students feared from her.

"I need to make an important announcement today." – she continued.

"I need to introduce you to a little girl. Her name is Shruti Singh. She is a student of Class-1st in our school."

"Yes madam." – all students spoke in a common voice.

"She is the little girl who says she has tied Rakhi to a tree- Neem tree in the garden of her house." – The Principal paused for a while.

9

Shruti was quiet but she was confused over what was happening. She had stopped crying now, because in between her father told her not to cry, and that he will handle and will make everything fine.

The principal came closer to Shruti and her parents, and asked the students, "What do you all think about it?"
Silence rose in the seminar room.

"It might be a joke. How can a tree be a human's brother?" – Rahul replied from Class-1st
"It's the funniest thing I have ever come to know." – Sushant from Class-3rd
"Any more answers from you all" – The principal asked.

The answers made her parents worried. They thought that the announcement might be a way to make fun of their daughter in front of the whole school.
The Principal then came back to the original place and said, "I just got the answers from you all. Now, I wish to ask the little girl about her experience with the tree."

She moved towards Shruti which made her more nervous. She tried to move backward but then Principal said her, "Shruti, come near to me. Don't fear. You tied the Rakhi as you say. How was your day?"

Shruti hesitatingly, glanced towards her father, who smiled and encouraged her to speak without fear, she then replied, "Madam, It was a very good day. My father clicked many pictures of mine with my brother tree. I also tied Rakhi to him. My brother is very nice. I love my brother so much".

Principal smiled at her and tapped her back and took the mike as she continued, "We all might think that this girl is crazy or so that she has developed affection with a tree. We are not wrong; things like this are so rare to see in this world. But, in fact this little girl is also not wrong."

Principal said as she turned to Shruti, "We, teachers teach the children about the moral sciences, science, social studies, etc. But this girl understood the basic of all these studies, and that is humanity. Her emotional attachment with the tree as she tied a Rakhi to it is a very important indication that this girl at a very little age possesses good emotions."

"Madam, I have a question to this." – Mrs. Priya, the English teacher raised a question.
The Principal thought for a short while. She then called the peon and said, "Take Shruti to the play section. Let her play for a while."

"My dear Shruti. Go to the Play section and play with toys for a while. We are having a discussion. We will call you over here when we are done." – The Principal whispered to Shruti.

The peon moved towards Shruti and in a short while, walked out with her to the play section of the school. Shruti was moving out but looking towards her parents who were still not well acquainted to the situation, somehow.

The Principal then turned towards the audience, and said, "Yes

Mrs. Priya. You can continue with your question."
Mrs. Priya continued "Madam, I would like to say that as we know she is treating it like her brother. But, it is not like one. It can't move. It can't play with her. She will one day realize that it is not like her real brother. Then what is the meaning of all this because at that stage it will make her sad."

The Principal calmly replied, "Mrs. Priya, your query is justifiable. I have studied Psychology in my Masters and what I conclude is that at this tender age, Shruti is full of emotions. At a later stage situations may arise as to what you pointed but these emotions will make the way then. It will pave the path to her emotional strength."

The Principal then pointed towards Shruti's parents, "Meet them. They are Mr. Pramod Singh & Mrs. Indra Singh, the parents of Shruti. They inspired and encouraged her to this decision."

"We would like to know what encouraged you to take such a decision for her?" – Mr. Rajesh the games teacher asked.
The Principal gave the mike to Shruti's father, he took it and replied, "The reason of encouragement is a long story.

Summarily, it's that we love her so much and we don't want to make her sad at any cost. We also don't want to beg anyone to let them allow my daughter to tie Rakhi to their son's hands and then accuse her of having interest in costly Rakhi gifts. Her father is alive and he is capable enough to fulfil her monetary needs. And lastly with this tree, we can ensure that it will be there even after my death with her."

The whole atmosphere becomes silent for a while. Everyone was getting emotional due to his statement. "This is what I would like to say. Thank you!" – as he ended his speech, the whole seminar room echoed with sounds of claps.

He handed over the mike back to the Principal and turned back to his original place on the stage. His wife Indra was feeling proud of him, and it was proven in form of the smile on her face & tears that made her eyes shine.

The Principal then continued, "As we have information, Mr & Mrs. Singh both are playing an important role in the Environmental Preservation. They were the couple who planted 151 saplings in the nearby barren sports club campus and turned it into an area of greenery."

The whole atmosphere echoed with the sound of claps. "Thank you so much for all this. It's a humble request to all of you. Please! Don't make fun of my daughter for this. She is sentimental and we can't see her sad."- Her father added.

The Principal marked the ending of the discussion, as she said, "So, now we are ending this discussion. I would like to instruct all the students that they will not tease Shruti for this from now onwards. If I receive any such complaint from her, that student will be severely punished for this. We are proud that she is a student of this school. Thank you! All students to move back to their classes with their respective class-teachers."

The seminar room was slowly emptying as the students moved out. Shruti's parents moved out with the Principal to the Principal room, where they saw Shruti sitting on the chair.
"Mummy" – she said and hugged her mother as she entered the Principal's room. Her mother too hugged her and made her comfortable.

"Listen Shruti. No need to worry. No one will tease you now. If someone teases you then you can directly complain to me. Are you happy now?" – The Principal said politely.

"Yes madam" – Shruti said as a smile grew on her face
Her parents also were quite relaxed to know that now their daughter will not be teased for this. They were also feeling proud of their daughter which made them proud in front of the whole school. Shruti was also happy to know that no one will tease her from now on. As a relaxation for the day, the Principal allowed Shruti to go home along with the parents for the day.

When they came from the school, her parents were happy to get their cheerful and happy daughter Shruti back. When their car reached the parking area of their house, Shruti came out of the car and walked to the Tree.

She went near to the parking lot and whispered to the tree, "I love you my brother. You know from now onwards no one will tease me. Principal ma'am told me that if anyone will tease me she will punish him. She also asked me about you" – she hugged the tree and narrated the whole happening to the tree.

After hugging the tree, when she turned back then she saw both her mother and father smiling and looking at her. She requested to click a photo of her with her brother, which they readily agreed. Obviously capturing pictures with family was indeed a thing which people mostly do during happy times. And now, it made their family complete too

10

Days, Months and Years went and now, the little Shruti turned to be a 17-year old descent and beautiful girl studying in a reputed convent school of the city. She now has a dream, the dream to become a medico. Her parents supported her views and wanted that she should achieve her target in any case.

"Mom, I am leaving for the school now." – Shruti said to her mother.
"Ok my princess. We have to go to Sharma uncle's house for the greh pravesh also. Do keep this in mind."

"Yes mom. The evening tuition will be over by 6pm and I will come home positively before 6.30pm." – She replied.
"Ok bye, my princess." – Her father said while reading the newspaper. It was his first and foremost work to enjoy reading the newspaper and then getting ready for the office.

"Bye papa." – Shruti said before leaving.
It was Shruti's regular habit to leave home 5minute early to spend the time with her brother the tree, taking care of it. The tree had reached its height as per the time span and also grew into a big tree as of now.

Shruti was standing near to the tree and whispering to it, "You know today, we will be having a small test and I am sure I will score high in that test. Please bless me my dear brother."

"Shruti, please come immediately. We are getting late." – Her

friend Muskaan said from outside of their house.
"Oh Yes. I am coming, Muskaan." – Shruti said as she moved hurriedly towards the gate.

Muskaan and Shruti were great friends as of now. She was along with Seema and other kids in the same school. After the instance, she felt bad about her approach in taunting Shruti about her brother tree.

On the other hand, Seema too did study with her till class 10th and then opted for Science and Mathematics as her subjects. Due to her father's transfer to Ambala, she had to go with them to the new city, where she sought admission into a new school.

She was also a friend with Shruti, however she boasted a lot which she didn't liked at all.
Shruti being big-hearted forgave her and with time their friendship grew deep and now they were very nice friends.

"Have you completed the assignment the biology teacher gave us?" – Muskaan asked.
"Yes, I have done that." – She replied confidently. She regularly studied and she did her assignment prior to the deadline to avoid last time rush.

And then they went together to the school. Muskaan and Shruti both reached the school on time. The class rushed to the assembly and then the first class.
"Oh, I forgot to bring the forceps for the experiment today. What should I do?" – Shruti got worried.

Just then Mrs. Bharti, the laboratory teacher announced, "Everyone keep your laboratory instrument box in front of you on the table. I am coming to each and every desk to find out

whether everyone brought their instruments or not."
Muskaan replied to her - "No problem, I will give it to you after I do the work and then after you are done with the work hand it over to me."

Shruti was not agreeing to it as there are fair chances that she would get caught for not bringing all the instruments needed for the biology practical class. But, she got convinced as nothing can be done except to inform the lecturer about the same, which could lead to scolding from the lecturer.

"Where did I forget it?" – She asked herself. She began to recall the last time she accessed the laboratory instrument box for the forceps and then she realized that she used it at home and may be forgot to keep it at the right place again.

"We don't have the time to think about it. Take it now, as madam is coming to you before checking my section. Hand it over to me after you are done with it."
"But that will be incorrect."
"Ok. Then be ready for the scolding. You know how much she scolds when students forgot to bring their instruments along with them."

Shruti remembered the last time when Mahesh forgot to bring the forceps. The teacher told him to move out of the laboratory and then insulted her in the next theory class too.
It's a sort of embarrassment if she admits she forgot to bring forceps. It is very important because it is needed to pick up sections of root, stem and leaves (TS and LS).

She was in her thoughts when the teachers arrived to her & asked, "Shruti Singh. Do you have all required instruments?"
"Madam" she whispered. Then she opened the instrument box

and closed her eyes in fear to be punished. She feared that now she will be definitely punished for not bring the important instrument and may be turned out of the class. She feared and due to this closed her eyes.

"Shruti" – a voice arosed. She opened the eyes to see that the teacher had move on to the other students for checking their instruments. She turned around to see that it was Muskaan's voice from the front desk and she was insisting to give the forceps back to her.

Shruti was saved from the scolding and she thanked Muskaan for the same. After the school got over, she came to her home and as usual she went to meet her brother the tree firstly before entering the house.

When she went inside the home, she came to know that a friend of her father (Ashutosh Uncle) had come to their house. He was with his wife Sapna Aunty and 5-year old son Chirag. They were talking and having tea. After greeting the guests, Shruti went to her room, changed her clothes and was about to sit for study, when her mother called up. She wanted her help in the kitchen to serve the guests.

When she went to the hall after helping her mother out in kitchen, Ashutosh uncle asked her, "What are you doing these days, Shruti?"
She replied, "I will be appearing for the board exams this year and also the Pre-medical tests for admission to medical colleges."

Her father's friend Ashutosh, who was a Mechanical Engineer with a well-known company in New Delhi was on a visit to his native place. He and Shruti's father graduated from the same college of the city.

He replied, "These days admission to the medical colleges is getting tougher day by day. Will you drop a year too, if you don't get selected this year?"

Her father replied, "Yes, we are thinking to get her admitted to a reputed coaching centre. They claimed many admissions this year."

Ashutosh uncle on listening the same replied, "Why to waste a year? If she gets admitted to the government college it's fine. Or else send her to abroad for pursuing her medical degree."

Shruti and her friends were disappointed to hear such an answer from her father's friend. He was getting directly negative on this.

"Why won't I get selected in the exam this year only. I will get selected" – she thought for a while.

Her father replied after a short while, "You are right on this concept of not wasting a year. But, education abroad is a big and costly deal. We are simple person living on a monthly salary. How can one afford lacs of fees each year?"

Listening to this Mrs. Sapna replied, "Education is quite costly but it saves year and one acquires a good qualification."

Her father's friend interrupted in between, "See. You have a prime location property in this city. You don't have to fear about it. There are some investors who will lease the front area of your property (.i.e. the garden area) and provide you a handsome yearly rent for it."

Shruti was not agreeing to them, but she was silent as her mother and father taught her not to speak when elders are talking with each other. Suddenly, she noticed that the 5-year old kid whose name was Chirag was running around and in between constantly scratching his legs, due to which the scratched area of the leg turned red.

She went to him and found that he has developed severe itching and rashes on the area that was been constantly scratched.
She pointed this to her father's friend, and he replied, "We have told him not to play outside but he doesn't obeys us. No need to worry, he will wash his leg and everything will be fine."

"It is eczema. It won't get away with washing. It is dermatitis" – Shruti replied
The child's mother seemed worried on listening that it may be dermatitis. She asked Shruti, "Do you have some remedy for it?"

"I have a natural remedy for it. Just wait, while I bring it" – Shruti said as she rushed outside the house.
"Sapna, There is no need of any remedy for it. It is normal." – Ashutosh uncle was still up with his opinion. Just then Shruti arrived with some neem leaves and went straight away to the kitchen. There she washed the leaves first and then made a paste of neem leaves and turmeric by grounding them.

She walked out of the kitchen with the paste and applied the paste on Chirag's leg and then tied it safely with a band-aid.
Sapna Auntie was quite happy to see Shruti's instant remedy for eczema and was also relieved because she knew that natural remedies also have a great action.

Chirag was feeling well now and so this relieved him too. They all had a good conversation for a while and then Ashutosh uncle and auntie went to their house.

AT THE DINNER TABLE

Shruti and her parents were sitting at the dining table and having dinner. All of them were silent. Her mother broke the silence and said to Shruti, "Sapna Auntie didn't say anything but she was quite happy to see how you cared about Chirag."

Shruti listened to her and replied, "Mom, he was suffering from eczema and in this condition, proper treatment need to be given. Uncle was not convinced till the end, but some things can't be taken in a normal way. It will further worsen the situation."

"Yes. You are right, Shruti. How's your preparation for the exam going on?" – Her father interrupted and asked.
"It's going on fine, dad. I need to concentrate on Physics more as the numerical questions need more and more practice." – She replied

Her father looked up to her and said, "Do try your best for the government exams. I am sure you will get admitted to a govt. Medical college. If not, we will think of some alternate solution"
Shruti looked upwards and asked, "Alternate solution? Is it the same as told by Ashutosh uncle."

Both her parents looked at her and then her father thought for a while and replied, "I don't think there is anything wrong with the solution. Leasing out property is a good solution. I want that you should fulfil your dreams, my princess."

Shruti looked at her parents, she was upset and about to cry, she replied, "And, I want that my brother tree should be taken care of, and it should be in the habitat which is most suitable for it .i.e. the present habitat."

"Why are you both father-daughter forecasting things so soon? My princess is intelligent enough to secure a seat in the government college. No need of sending her abroad. Isn't she?" – Her mother interrupted in their conversation. She did know that this conversation will end in a conclusion that would hurt either of them.

"Yes, my princess is very intelligent. She will definitely make us proud for sure." – Her father also agreed.

11

Days and weeks went by and finally the exam dates came out. Shruti tried her level best to score good marks in the exams. She scored good marks in the board exams and finally the result of the Pre medical examinations were going to be declared.

The phone rang. Her mother came and picked the phone up.
"Auntie, I want to talk with Shruti." It was Muskaan on the other line.
"Yes Muskaan, just wait for a second."- She said as she called Shruti. Her tone was lower as usual. Usually when she called then she used to be delighted but this time the talk was straight away.

Shruti came around hurriedly and took the phone and started talking. Her mother was worried as both of them appeared for the pre medical examination.
"When did the result came out? I checked the website early morning."

This question raised by Shruti confirmed to her mother that the talk is about a recent result in the pre medical examination. Her mother stood there to listen about the talk.
"How much is the cut-off?" – She asked

"Ok. Let me check it on my computer. I will call you later bye."
– Shruti ended the call and rushed to her room. Her mother followed her to her room.

"Are the results out?" – Her mother asked

"Yes mom. I am checking about my result"

"Don't be anxious. Everything will be good." – Her mother said as she saw nervousness of Shruti as she switched on the laptop.

Shruti stared at the computer screen and entered her roll numbers when prompted by the website. Both of them were silent. The sound of the ceiling fan could also be clearly heard due to the silence that rose in the house.

"What happened? Are you selected?"

"Cut-off is 180/200 and my score is 178. I am not selected." – Shruti replied sadly

"Oh. That's so sad" – Her mother also became a bit sad. She knew that it was Shruti's childhood dream to become a doctor and PMTs being the entry level exam meant a lot as they allow one to pursue the 5½ years course to become a doctor.

"What about Muskaan?"

"She got selected with rank 1209"

"You and dad expected a lot from me regarding this exam but I couldn't get through. I am very sorry to both of you mom. I failed." – Shruti said and started crying.

"Don't cry. My princess doesn't deserve crying. She is strong enough and intelligent enough to find her way. You have not failed; you were just unable to clear the exam." – Her mother hugged her and consoled her. It's the parents who can console a kid when he/she gets emotionally distressed.

Inside the heart, her mother feared too that if she is not getting through her father may go with the decision to send her abroad which will mean she will have to move away from her parents and her brother tree.

Her mother on the other hand, was also very much disturbed as she had never stayed away from her daughter and it will be very hard, if her father goes by the decision which he forecasted many days before.

The door bell rang. It was her father who had just arrived. Her mother went to open the door and as usual her father came with a joyful mood but sooner by seeing the sadness on face of her mother, he anticipated that something is wrong.

He asked Indra, "What happened? Is everything fine?"
"Should I bring a cup of tea for you?" – Indra replied. She was not having the courage to announce this sad news to him.
"Firstly, I need to know that what happened when I was outside. Did anyone say anything to you?" – Her father asked.

"All India PMTs results are out" – Her mother said.
Now, her father got serious. He now realised the reason why she was upset. He pre-estimated that what could be the result but still asked "What is the result?"
"2 marks less then cut-off marks" – her mother replied

Her father became silent and did not speak a word then. He moved to the living room and sat down. Both the mother and the daughter were worried about him and walked behind him to the room.
"I am sorry, dad. Your princess couldn't fulfil your expectations." – Shruti said and tears began to flow from her eyes.

"Don't be sad, my princess. I can't see you sad. Your father is alive now. Don't cry my princess." – Her father said while he tried to console her. She hugged him and both of them got emotional.

He then sat down on the chair and her mother brought a glass of water for him. He drank it and began to think for a while.

"I think we should plan for her studies now. I have come up with a thought, Indra. I think that will be fine for all of us."

"What are you thinking of?" – Her mother asked impatiently. She wanted to know that what was going in his mind.

"I think we should think about Ashutosh's proposal. I will ask Ashutosh about the arrangements to be made for the abroad admissions." – Her father said.

"You are thinking of sending her abroad. How will she stay over there? How will we stay here without her" – Her mother grew emotional.

"Secondly I can't live without her. She has never gone to another city alone and now, another country? No." – She added.

Her father was also feeling sad. It was just a talk of sending her abroad but it made him worried too. As a father, he always wanted to secure his kid each and every way. His view was that parent's responsibility is not limited to financially support their kids but to emotionally support them and gradually strengthen them to face the world as well as to guide them to achieve the highest possible achievement and qualifications.

At times it may include taking strict decisions too, but those decisions that will have a good long-term impact.

"What is your opinion? It's your career and your decision is the most important." – Her father asked Shruti.

"I will not go abroad for the medical course. I don't want to pursue my dreams at the cost of this house." – Shruti announced immediately.

"Look, my princess. You will have to pursue your dreams. We

know it's your childhood dream to become a medico. Secondly, we are not selling it out. It will be just a lease." – Her father replied.
Shruti's inner thought was that if she were given a second chance then she will definitely get selected with a good rank.

"Okay. I give you some time to think over this. But, in any case your decision should be final. And, I want that you should never have to regret for this decision later. So, decide very carefully."
"Ok dad."

Her father took up the phone and dialled a number. Shruti could not figure out the number but she thought it might probably be Ashutosh uncle.
"Hello Ashutosh, Pramod here. How are you"
"I am fine. You tell Pramod, how are you doing?" – Ashutosh uncle replied.

"I would like to meet you and discuss about the lease proposal you talked about and the medical colleges abroad." – He added
"Sure, come over my house in the half an hour. We will surely meet and discuss all prospects. I have the guidance booklets and the director of a college is my friend." – Ashutosh on the other side.

"Ok. I am coming in the next half an hour to meet you. Take care. Bye!" – Her father replied and ended the conversation.
Shruti and her mother looked at each other when her father ended the conversation. The whole atmosphere of the house became silent for a while. Just then, Shruti took the courage and said, "Papa, I would like to prepare for a year. I don't want to go away from you all."

Her mother too gathered the courage now, and said, "Give her one chance. I am sure she will secure a good rank in the PMTs and secure a position in the city college itself."

Her father looked at her and replied peacefully, "Your one year is precious for me. I also don't want to send you abroad for studies for a period of 5½ years but I myself am bound. I want your success at any cost, my princess"

Shruti looked at her father. She could find that he is correct. She remembered how he took so much care of her, like a protective and affectionate person. He was her protective shield. If we talk out generally, then also Father is a caring and protective shield for their children.

Shruti's father seemed to be committed enough for her career. As a father, his expectations were not wrong, also.

"I am going to meet Ashutosh. I might be late, so both of you have dinner and then take rest." – Her father replied while he got up to leave for his friend's house.

Shruti was quiet. She was not saying anything but she wanted to convince her father, but she knew that her father's decision is usually the final decision.

"Close the door." – her father called from outside.

Shruti got up and closed the door. Her mother was in kitchen and busy in preparing vegetables for the dinner.

Shruti came near to her and asked, "Mummy why is dad in much hurry? I have appeared for the state level exam too, whose result is still not out."

Her mother who was quiet for a while, took her hand in hand and said, "My doll, I know you are quite concerned about us and don't want to leave us but things go this way only. Regarding your exam results, I will talk with your father. Don't be tensed."

12

Shruti was convinced with what her mother said, because she did knew that her mother was a bold lady and Shruti did knew how to handle such situations.

Just then the phone rang. It was Seema on the other side.
"Hi! Shruti, how are you? I came to know that the result had been declared. How were the results?" – She directly inquired about the results, which hinted Shruti that she knows the result prior and talking just to confirm it.

"Hmm I secured 2 marks less then the cut-off marks, hence not selected" – she replied sadly and tiredly.
It was a matter of tiredness more then sadness these days, when numerous of her known ones called her to inquire about the result.

"Oh. Thats so sad. Well, I have secured admission in a good college here. I will be getting my favourite branch Computer Sciences hopefully." – She said proudly, which confirmed that the conversation was to boast herself.
"And, what about Muskaan? She also appeared in the examination." – She asked.

"Thats good. Congratulations. Muskaan has got selected with rank 1209 but the name of the college is not decided yet. It may be any place in India"
"Doing M.B.B.S is a great thing. She will get a good position. So, I was planning a visit to the city. We all will meet up and

have fun." – She announced happily.

"Ok. That is a good thing." – She tried to be normal.
"Isn't it exciting? We all friends will be together after two complete years. We all will have great fun together."

Shruti was getting bored with this stuff. She did know that Seema usually calls her to tell her whereabouts rather than to ask hers.
"Seema, my mother is calling me in the kitchen. I will call you back later" – Shruti said so as to end the conversation.

"Okay. I will tell you when I come. Bye"
"Bye" – she said and was quite relieved. She ended up the conversation and sat on the chair near the dining table.

Her mother was in kitchen came near to her and said, "You will have to face these things. Be strong." Shruti looked at her mother and replied - "I know mom. I try to handle these things patiently. But you don't know her. She always boasts and behaves as if I am inferior and she is superior."

She was a bit angry to see people asking out for her results every now and then. Everyone including the neighbours was quite keen in asking about her results which made it even more depressive for her. She tried hard and exams were okay but she couldn't make it as the cut-offs were also quite high.

"I don't know her but I know my princess will handle the situation perfectly." – Her mother replied calmly and then got up.

"I am preparing my princess's favourite dish for her and it will take her anger and sadness away" she added and went to the kitchen. She wanted to make her happy as she knew she was quite upset from the moment, the result was out.

Shruti was just thinking when the thought of the decision came into her mind. Her father told her to take a final decision. For Shruti it was a tough decision to take. If she agrees, it will put her house on lease and she will have to get away from her mother, father and her brother tree for a big time period of 5½ years.

On the other hand her mother was troubled because she thought that if they have to send her abroad then how she will be able to manage things over there.
Her mother wanted to clarify these things with her father at the first place but then she thought that it may not be the appropriate to discuss it in front of her as it will loosen her self-confidence if finally she decides to go abroad where she will have to manage things on her own.

Her father was also concerned. During driving also, he was thinking about the future decision of Shruti. He was also worried but as he was the decision maker of the family he made himself strong. At times, one needs to take tough decisions, which will be beneficial for the family in long-span.

The day ended with the whole family of three concerned and tensed about the issue that arose just now. Her father and mother and she herself didn't have a good time.

NEXT DAY

The next morning, her mother woke up at 05.00am. She stood up and was cutting vegetables sitting on the chair near the dining table. On seeing the lights on, her father got up and came to the hall.

"Indra, you got up quite early today. I know you might have not slept quite well the last night." – He said as he saw her sitting on the chair.

"You also didn't sleep well. I know this. When the child is worried and sad, how can parents get a good sleep?" – Her mother replied.

"Where is Shruti?" – He asked.

"She also didn't sleep properly. I convinced her and made her sleep at 02am." – Her mother said.

"What does she say about her future plans?" – Her father asked

"No, she hasn't decided yet. She told that she was expecting a good result out of this exam but the result was opposite to her expectations." – Her mother replied.

"Hmm. Competition is quite tougher these days. She is quite hard working and that I know." – Her father said.

"Yes. I remember that she revised everything 2-3 times before appearing for the examination." – Her mother said.

Her father came near to the dining table and sat on another chair. On seeing this, her mother said, "I am going to prepare cup of tea for you" and stood up to go to the kitchen.

"Please don't go. I need to talk to you for a while." – Her father requested.

Her mother turned around and asked, "I also want to talk with you."

"Yesterday, I talked with Ashutosh regarding the admission to medical courses abroad and he told me about two of the best colleges." – Her father spoke as her mother got seated on the chair close to her father's.

"Ok. How much will be the expenditure?" – Her mother replied. She was quit impatient to know the expenditure as they will have to be financially equipped before sending their daughter abroad.

Her father said, "See, I will arrange for it. Don't care about the money".
Her mother looked at her husband's face, and asked, "I want to know exactly how much we will have to arrange?"

Her father took a deep breath and replied, "5 lacs for the admission and after a month 3 lacs as the yearly fees."
"How will we, afford this much money? 8 lakhs is not simply an easy game."

Her father said to her, "We talked with a person on phone. He will be coming to see the property today for lease purpose. Ashutosh assured me that on confirmation, he will pay a good amount per month along with nearly 6 lacs advance."
"And, how will we arrange the rest 2 lacs?"

Her father replied in convincing way, "We will simply pay them Rs.5 lacs for admission and then we have 1 month for arrangement of Rs.2 lacs. I will take a loan if nothing happens."
"Things will go complicated this way. Do you think we will be able to manage things?" – Her mother asked. She was concerned to know about expenditure and that how they will arrange the money for Shruti's studies abroad.

"If things don't work out as I devised, I will do some alternate arrangements. We have a joint Rs.3 lacs FD which we got when Shruti was 3year old. I will surrender it to arrange money."

Indra was sad on hearing this. This money which they invested as FD was for Shruti's marriage. This was the security for which she was confident that a few arrangements for her daughter's marriage will be done with this amount.

"We planned it for her marriage. And, then how will we arrange for her marriage?" – Her mother reminded her father.
"Our first duty towards her is to provide her with quality education." – Her father replied
"Yes that is true."

The discussion ended with the arrival of the newspaper hawker. Their newspaper hawker used to ring their bell to make them know that the newspaper has arrived. When Pramod was about to leave for the office, the phone rang, "Hello, Pramod Singh speaking. Who is this?"

"Hello I am Mr. Shashikant. Mr. Ashutosh told me to contact you. I want to take a land on lease. I think he has talked to you about this." – The person on the other end spoke.
"Yes, it's under my ownership."
"We want to see it today in an hour."

"Presently, I am about to leave for my office. I will show the land in the evening."
"Ok Mr. Singh. We will meet in the evening. I will come along with Mr. Ashutosh sharp at 06pm. Will it be ok?"
"Ok fine. We will meet at that time surely" – Her father said and ended the conversation.

Her father was a bit happy to know this, as he was thinking that it will lead to arrangement of money easily if things work out in this way.

13

He turned around and took his bag and continued to walk towards the door as he saw her mother in front of him.

"They are coming today to see the land. Let's see if they like it. I am quite confident that everything will be arranged automatically for my princess's education. I will not let anything hinder it." – Her father said confidently.

"But what about the greenery we have in front of our house. That will be surely cut down."

"We will have to sacrifice something to attain something. And may be in the future she turns out to be a good doctor and buy a big farm house where they will be only and only greenery. Have a broader approach, Indra." – Her father said in a way as to convince her mother.

He too was an environmental lover but for him, as of now his daughter was the first priority and for it, he could do anything.

IN THE EVENING

A black coloured Mercedes car stopped at the gate of her house with blowing of a horn. Pramod guessed it was Mr. Shashikant. He also arrived at his home only an hour ago, as he knew that Mr. Shashikant will be coming at 6pm.

He rushed to the drawing room to be sure everything was well arranged. And then he rushed to the gate of the house. He saw the car standing outside the house.

He went close and could see that a person in grey coloured suit came out of the car.

"Hello Sir, pleased to meet you?" – Her father greeted the person.

"No I am not. There is a confusion. Shashikant ji is in the car sitting in the back seat." – The person said

Just then the gate opened and a tall 40-something person came outside the car. He was quite handsome and looked very nice in the black coloured coat and white T-shirt.

"Hello, Is it Mr. Singh?" – the gentleman asked

"Yes. I am Mr. Pramod Singh." – her father introduced himself

"So, this is the property. How much is the dimensions of the property?"

"The whole land including the house is 90X90"

"Oh I see. Good size."

"Can I see the property? I would like to see if it suits our project or not." – the person asked

"Yes sure. But, where is Ashutosh?" – Her father asked looking around for his friend.

"Here I am." – Ashutosh said. He had just arrived, amidst the discussion between Shashikant and Pramod Singh.

"I would like to see the whole property. I am quite interested in the location" – Mr. Shashikant put forward his wish to visit the whole property .i.e. the back garden and the total house from outside.

"Offcourse sir. But, we need to...." – He was interrupted by Ashutosh as he said, "Yes."

Pramod Singh wanted to confess that he doesn't have any plan to sell the property but to simply lease the front land. Pramod

Singh was quite astonished to see how Ashutosh interrupted but he stayed silent.

"Ok. It's a very nice property. I am thinking to finalize the deal now." – Mr. Shashikant said after viewing the whole property.
"That is very nice. As per the market rate as of now, the lease rate will be decided by the real estate consultant. Is it ok with you?" – Her father replied.

Mr. Shashikant thought for a while, as he was standing near the lobby of the house. He then said, "Well Mr. Singh, we are quite interested in this property. I want to buy this whole property and would like to build a commercial project over here."

Pramod Singh replied, "Sorry Sir, but that is the property which I inherited from my grandfather. I can't sell it off, but I will be interested in the lease of the front land. 30x90"
Pramod Singh never even dreamt to sell or mortgage the property. He even never considered it as an alternate arrangement for her education. Selling the property inherited from his father was never the thing he thought of.

"Mr. Singh first of all let us tell you the amount as per the market rates. As I enquired, the market rate comes in the range of 7 crores for this property."
"7 crores is a big sum, Pramod. You can think of it." – Ashutosh suggested.

"I can't think about selling it. It's very important for me and my family. It's our parental house."
"Mr. Singh, my deal is at 8 crores plus a 3BHK flat at ABC Plaza just opposite to Mr. Ashutosh's house. Now tell me are you interested?" – He proposed.
"Wow, that's nice. ABC plaza is just opposite to the building in

which I have my flat. That will be a superb location. Think once about this exciting offer, Pramod." – Ashutosh said happily

Pramod Singh was not able to think about the offer. He himself knew how he convinced himself about the lease. And now the offer of sale was completely unaccepted by his inner self. Additionally, no one will be convinced in the family also.

Mr. Shashikant told him good bye and went leaving him with an offer that made his mind and inner-self to argue with one another. Mind was saying that the offer is very nice and to go for it, while the inner-self was stick on the fact that the house was a memory of his forefathers and it was the best place to live in for him and his family.

Ashutosh said, "Pramod you should think about the offer. Look, sometimes some of our decisions can change our entire life. Think of it."
"Ashutosh, you know how much we are attached to this house. Shruti is very much attached to her brother 'Neem'. How will it be possible?"

"I know this but in fact, this is once in a lifetime opportunity. Think of it. I have to go now." – Ashutosh replied as he stepped outside the house. After saying good bye to Ashutosh, Pramod singh came in and sat near the tree.

He knew that Shruti and her mother will not agree to sell the house but it was in fact a good offer to go with. It will make them financially strong and a 3BHK flat at no cost to them is simply an addon to the 8cr offer.

He was thinking that how come things get complex in life and we have to choose between two things.

"Dad, what are you doing? Are you talking with my brother?" –

The sudden voice of Shruti made him came out of his thoughts and he began to look up and found Shruti standing close to the place where he was sitting. Coincidently he was sitting near to the tree.
"My princess, come here." – He called her calmly.
"Yes dad."

Her father asked her in a caring way, "My princess, Are you angry at me that I am thinking to send you abroad for medical studies?"
Shruti got somehow serious and replied, "I am not angry, dad. But, I don't want you and our house to suffer due to all this. I asked a friend about lease. These people change the land to commercial place and then gain from it."

"They will cut the trees and construct a big building over here and then earn from it. I don't want to lose my brother or its habitat." – She added. It seemed that she was quite serious about the issue and that's why she inquired with her friends about this.

Her father looked at her. Her way of expression of thoughts made it quite clear that she wasn't self centred but cared for her parents and 'brother' too.
"But, if this leads to enable you to complete your dream education and accomplish your dreams it will be a good sacrifice. Isn't it?" – Her father tried to convince her.

She was about to say something when her mother came outside and asked, "So the father-daughter duo is sitting over here. When did you came, Shruti?"
"10 minutes ago, mom" – Shruti replied

"What did they say?" – Her mother asked her father.

Her father hinted her mother to be silent and to discuss the things later. Shruti saw the hinting but kept silent as she knew that she should not interfere in between issues, in which her parents don't want her involvement.

Her mother said "I want things to be clear because why did they see the whole property. Is it because.." – Her father interrupted "Indra, if you want it to be discussed then we will discuss it in house." -   Her father replied.

14

AT THE DINING TABLE

"Now please tell why did they see the whole property?" – her mother asked

"First promise that you won't be angry."

"Yes ok" – she replied instantly.

"Ok. Mr. Shashikant is the MD of the company who got ABC plaza constructed in front of Ashutosh's building."

"Ok. It's a very big building."

"Yes, He wanted to take a building on lease and visited us. Now, he gave me an offer to sell this whole house."

"sell? Are you planning to sell it?" – Her mother said impatiently.

"No. I am not agreeing. He has given us an offer – 8 crores and a 3BHK flat in the ABC Plaza in exchange for this property."

"No papa, we will not sell this property. I don't want to lose my brother tree and my dream house is this. Please dad, don't sell it." – Shruti requested as she was present over there and allowed to take part in the conversation.

Her father turned to her and said, "I never thought of selling the house but"

"But?" – Her mother asked

"But the offer will equip up with financial resources for your whole medical education in a top US university." – Her father explained.

"But, I don't want to do it this way, dad. I can't sacrifice my brother for it, dad?" – Shruti replied.

"You don't understand the complexities of the future, my child. Things are not so easy." – Her father said
"Dad, my decision is final. If you want me to join a university I will prefer joining a B.Sc course rather then anything at cost of my brother and our house." – Shruti said boldly

This was the first time when she said boldly in front of her parents. She loved her brother and her parents a lot and couldn't afford to lose them.

Days went by and this way a week passed.
A morning, the phone rang, her father picked the phone up. It was Ashutosh on the other end.
"Hello Pramod, how are you doing?"
"I am fine. You tell" – her father replied.
"Mr Shashikant called me to inquire about the offer he gave to you."

"Well, Ashutosh. Shruti has replied with a 'No' to the selling of the house." – Her father said clearly.
"Pramod, you are the decision maker or Shruti? You should clearly tell her about your decision. Some strict decisions need to be taken by you for the better future of the family." – Ashutosh replied

Her father didn't know what to say and so kept silent. He ended the conversation and thought for a while.
Just then, Shruti came up with a paper in hand. At that time, her father was sitting on the sofa thinking of the decision to be taken.

"Dad, please sign this application form."
"What application form is this?" – Her father asked.
"Application form for admission to B.Sc course" – Shruti said calmly.

"What? Are you serious?" – Her father asked.
"Yes dad. I am thinking to take admission in this course as it's your final decision that I should join a college just now." – Shruti replied

Her father got full of anger. Then he controlled himself as he realised that teenage children need to be handled calmly.
"Why do you want to do a B.Sc? I know your dream is to become a medico"
"Yes Dad, my dream is to be a doctor. But, I want to fulfil this dream in my own way and in my own country rather than going abroad. I don't want to be a medico with my house, my brother and my family at stake."

Just then Shruti's phone beeped. She looked up to see the message and she rushed to her room.
Her father didn't understand anything and asked, "What happened Shruti, where are you going?"

When she didn't answer, then he thought that maybe she might have gone for studying in her room.
He threw a glance at the newspaper and began to read it.
"Ohh an accident. These days' people are not careful while driving. Such carelessness lead to such accidents." – Her father murmured and turned to the next news.

"Mom-Dad, please come here." – Shruti said in a loud voice from inside her room suddenly
Her mother who was in kitchen rushed and her father both

came to her room anxiously.

"What happened, Shruti?" – Her father asked

"Dad, Muskaan messaged me about the result. And here is it. I got selected, dad." – Shruti said excitedly and hugged her father.

Her father gazed towards the laptop screen and found, "3rd rank in the state" – he said.

"What? Is it true?" – Her mother asked

"Yes Indra. She has done it. She got All state rank 3rd. Wow!" – Her father said and his face glowed with a magical smile .i.e. the smile of victory.

All the family members were very happy to hear this news as now she will not have to go away from her parents and her brother.

Just then something came in her father's mind as he said "This calls for a celebration. We will definitely go to a restaurant and have a great treat over there"

Her mother's happiness knew no bounds as she came to know that her daughter topped the state examination with the 3rd rank. Now they will not have to send her daughter to an unknown country thousand miles away from them.

"Will she get the city college MBBS seat?" – Her mother asked

"Sure. With the 3rd rank in the state, she will surely get the college she wishes for in the state." – Her father replied.

All the three got ready and were about to leave for the restaurant. It was 8p.m and just then the door bell rang.

"Who might have come at this moment?" – Her mother asked.

"Let us discover it by opening the gate." – Her father replied.

A 25-26yr old men was standing outside the gate. When they opened the gate, he introduced himself, "Madam, I am Anil from the TV News. I would like to meet and congratulate Miss Shruti Singh on her great success in the State PMT."

This was a start of the press and media arriving at the Singh's house for interviewing the family's topper in the state PMTs.
The whole family was so glad to receive a great response from the media and press.

They were hungry but didn't felt it because the happiness phase subsided the hunger for the three of them.
"This was the happiest day as it ended well." – Her father said his mother when the media and press people went after the interviews.

"Yes. But, what about the deal, which the builder offered us" – Her mother asked curiously.
Her father happily replied, "Now I can proudly deny to their offer. We are financially able to handle the expenditure that will be incurred when she studies in the city medical college."

"That is very nice. I am so happy and she also is very happy about the same." – Her mother replied.
"Where is she now?" – Her father asked
"As usually, she is celebrating her success with her brother. She is sitting near to her brother and discussing with it. I don't know what answers she gets from the tree?" – Her mother said

"She cares about her brother since childhood. And, now even when she understands that it is a tree but still her care has not reduced in these years. This thing is the most important of all. Isn't it?" – Her father replied in a proud manner.

"Yes. We should be proud of her as she cares about the environment. Even she was thinking to sacrifice her dream

career for the sake of us and the tree." – Her mother said
"You know Indra, when we do something good then we end up with good things that happen to us. Mother nature is very kind and returns every good deed-small or large done to it." – Her father replied

"Yes you are correct. If everyone realises it and pledges to take care of the nature, then the world will be greener and better." – Her mother said

THE NEXT DAY

The family got up early in the morning and then decided to pay a visit to the deity which they believed a lot in. All the newspaper and local news channels were displaying the news of Shruti's success and she became the Topper icon of the city as of now.

Phone calls from known persons flooded as the news displayed on the newspapers and the TV screens.
One came from the co-worker at her father's office, who congratulated the whole family and wished them the best in the future too.

"Shruti, you made us proud. See the newspaper and the TV news channels, everywhere it's you and just you" – Her father said her which made her delighted
"Dad, I would like to say something. Can I?" – Shruti requested
"Yes sure, my princess." – Her father replied and her mother was sitting near them.

"Mom and Dad, I request you that don't sell the house or lease it now. Please it's a request. I can't see the house's natural habitat turn into a commercial place." – Shruti said in a requesting manner.

Her father said to her, "Listen my princess, we were thinking of leasing the property for a better future of yours. And now, that you have secured a good position; we don't need to do it now. Don't worry. I will deny to the offer."

Shruti smiled and felt relieved when she heard what her father told. She was feeling thankful to the god that she protected her house and her brother.

AFTERNOON

The door bell ranged. Shruti's mother got up to open the gate. Shruti was enjoying viewing TV in the living room. She usually opened the gate but these days due to the grand result she got, she got some privileges and relaxations too. She continued on watching TV yet paying attention to the one who have arrived.

Now, she could hear the conversation and thought some known ones have arrived. "Indra, you remember me?" – a female voice spoke.

"How can I forget you" – it was her mother's voice who replied to it.

"Indra, you forgot us these years. But, we couldn't. We miss you very much." – said the male voice

"I too miss you bhaiya. I didn't tie Rakhi to anyone else after that." – her mother replied.

Shruti was now able to realize that her mother is definitely talking with her maternal uncle. But as her mother told her previously that she had three maternal uncles, which one of them is him, she wondered.

She began to think and then, she heard the male voice again –

"Where is Shruti? She has made everyone of us feel proud. Where is my niece?"

On being asked about her, Shruti got up and made sure everything in the room is in its place and organised.
Just then her mother replied, "She is watching T.V right now." And called her, "Shruti, come here."

Shruti by now had realized that it was her maternal uncle and her aunt who have come to meet her. She was shy and confused what to tell them, but following her mother's call she stood up and went to the front hall of the house.
"So, this is Shruti, my niece." – Her uncle said. Shruti came and as a tradition touched their feet as a symbol to give regards to him.
"Yes. Her photo is there in all the newspapers today." – Her aunt replied.

"Bless you my child" – Her uncle said.
"Shruti, you know who I am?" – Her uncle asked
"Shruti, he is Shailesh uncle, your youngest maternal uncle." – Her mother interrupted and replied.

Shruti was quite happy to know that her youngest maternal uncle has come to meet her after a long time. But, she was still thinking, why after this much long time. Her mother used to tell her that all her three brothers love her a lot, then why this much time?
"You will be this generation's first doctor when you complete the course." – Shailesh uncle said proudly.
"Mummy, I should call dad also. He will be glad to meet Shailesh uncle." – Shruti said

When Shruti said that, Shailesh uncle's face turned down. He was looking as if he is disagreeing to Shruti. Her mother too looked at Shruti and then said her, "Your dad is very busy at the office. He will meet some other day."

Just then her mother realized that she hasn't brought anything to serve in front of them. She stood up and went to the kitchen. Shailesh uncle and aunt insisted that they don't want anything but it's a usual way that whenever someone comes to the house then we have to offer him/her something.

"Do you know you have a cousin brother, you can tie Rakhi to on Rakshabandhan?" – Her uncle said
Shruti looked at him in confusion but then replied calmly, "I have a brother I tie Rakhi to. It will be nice to tie an additional Rakhi to the cousin brother too."

"You have a brother? Where is he?" – Her aunt asked shockingly, as she knew that Shruti was the only child to her sister-in-law and they also don't have good relations with their in-laws and their kids.
"It's there just near to the main gate of this house, the grand big Neem tree. That tree is my brother" – Shruti replied proudly.

Shruti was a proud sister of the tree and she never got embarrassed or felt that tying Rakhi to a tree is a pity task. She was indeed proud to tie the Rakhi to her 'brother'.
"A tree! So you tie a Rakhi to a tree? You poor girl! You didn't have a brother and so you had to resort to a tree on Rakshabandhan?" – Shailesh uncle said.

These lines by Shailesh uncle did hurt her as well as her mother. She never expected such hurting lines from her uncle. She could remember each and every Rakshabandhan when her mother got three Rakhis but couldn't tie them to anyone.

She replied, "Shailesh uncle, I love my brother a lot. It is very special for me, because it doesn't have an attitude and never did deny me to tie Rakhi to it. Alike human beings, it is peace loving and contributes a lot to the nature."

Shailesh uncle got very angry to listen it as he thought these were directed to him, he anyways controlled her anger and replied, "So you think that tree is just like a brother. Tell me, Can a tree protect you? Can a tree help you out with anything?"

15

Seeing this discussion, between both of them, Shruti's mother tried to end it up by interrupting. She said "Shailesh bhai, Take biscuits and enjoy them till I am getting the tea done."
Shruti understood her mother's hint that she wants the conversation to end peacefully. So, she didn't reply to the question raised by her uncle.

Her uncle spoke further, "I know you don't have answers to it. A tree is a tree and can't replace a human being."
This statement of her uncle persuaded Shruti, who was till that time silent. She replied, "I have the answer to the same. A tree can protect us and the environment from global warming.

Green house gases are very hazardous and trees absorb the green house gas carbon-dioxide to protect us."
She added, "And I agree to your point, Shailesh uncle that tree can't replace a human being but side by side a human being too can't replace a tree."

This time Shruti's mother didn't say or hinted anything to Shruti. She knew that Shruti usually respected elders but when elders are incorrect and still want to dominate then things need to be sorted out.

Shailesh uncle also realised by now that his niece Shruti is very confident and fixed in her views and her views can't be altered.
After a few minutes, bell rang again. Shruti looked at the clock and estimated who can be there at that moment.

"Let me see." – Shruti said while she stood up and rushed to the door to see.

She went and saw a boy standing at the door. He was wearing goggles and blue t-shirt and jeans, overall modern in appearance.

She asked, "Who is this?"

The one who was wearing goggles answered, "I am Saarthak and I want to meet Indra buaa, who lives here."

Shruti realized that this should be her cousin who came to meet her mother who was his buaa (paternal aunt).

"Who is there, Shruti?" – Her mother asked and arrived at the gate.

"Buaa, I am Saarthak." – The young boy replied when Shruti was about to say anything.

Her mother smiled and tears rolled down her cheeks. She hugged Saarthak and said, "Oh. When I last saw you, you were very small and now you have turned into a young handsome boy."

Saarthak also smiled a bit, but didn't tell anything.

Then Saarthak came to the hall where his mother and father were sitting on the sofa.

"Saarthak, you have come. You went to your friend's house nearby. Got your work done?" –Shailesh uncle asked.

"Yes dad." – He replied.

Saarthak sat on the sofa along with his father.

"So, what is he doing these days?" – Her mother asked.

"He has done her 10+2 and pursuing Engineering from the regional college." – His mother replied.

Saarthak glanced at Shruti and then asked, "If I am not wrong, she is Shruti?"

"Yes, I am Shruti. It's nice to meet you." – Shruti replied almost instantly.

Saarthak said, "I have seen today's newspaper and all are flooded with your success story of cracking the state PMT. You are the shining star of the family. You must be feeling proud of yourself."

"There is no need to feel proud. I feel happy that I got my dreams and my family's expectations fulfilled." – Shruti replied confidently.

"Do you play video games?" – He asked

"No" – She replied.

"You always think of video games. Did you ask about her examination strategy? You will be appearing for CAT after degree. It's fully a competitive exam." – Shailesh uncle said to Saarthak.

Shruti looked and observed Saarthak. He got a mix of sad+anger on being told so by his father.

"What you do in your leisure time?" – He asked.

"I usually go out in my front garden and have a great time over there seeing greenery and observing the natural habitat."

"So you are a tree lover, right?"

"Yup, I love trees. More specifically I am an environment or nature lover, you can say." – She illustrated.

"Is there a job option as Environmentalist with this interest of yours?"

"Not every interest can be monetized. Some are simply your passion. You like to do these things and so you do it."

Saarthak was left with no option other then to say "Yes" to it. It was clear with these things to Saarthak and his parents that Shruti had well-defined thoughts about her interests and her affections. It was not a whimsical decision of her, to simply call a tree as her brother.

As expected by her mother, Shailesh uncle and his family went before Shruti's father was back to home. She knew that he will not like her brother's entry to their home and will take it the wrong way.

In the evening, Shruti went near to the tree. It was the place where she sorted out small and big problems or confusions which she had. It was in fact that she felt confident in making out decision at that place, which seemed like a big problem usually. She usually did that when she was confused.

Shruti was suspicious about the sudden arrival of Shailesh uncle and his family to their home after a long period of time. She thought to ask her mother but on seeing happiness on her face after meeting her brother after a long span of time, she didn't have the courage to ask her.

It was not that she was unhappy to see them but the warmth and care she expected from a relative meeting after such a long time didn't happen in this case. Instead, Shailesh uncle and his son Saarthak bombarded her with question about the tree. Yes, she would appreciate Shailesh's uncle wife who was quiet on the issue.

Just then she observed that her father had arrived. She pretended to be normal because she knew that her father will know that she is sad and that her mother will get angry with her as she instructed her not to say anything about Shailesh uncle's to her father. Her mother told that if deemed necessary, she (her mother) herself will tell it to her father.

Anyways, things went on smoothly and the day also went smoothly. At the dining table her father was expressing her happiness over the compliments and praises received from the known ones in the office on the grand success of Shruti in the state PMTs.

Shruti was very excited and a bit nervous to know which college will be allotted to her. Her first preference surely was the regional city college. In addition to being situated in the heart of the city, it was the No.1 College of the state too. Now, she was eagerly waiting for the counselling to be held for allotment of the college.

Days went by and this way one month went away. The day of counselling came and everyone in the family was anxious regarding the allotment of college. Her mother and father were quite confident about the allotment of the regional college but she was a bit nervous.

"Be confident, my princess. You will surely get the college of your choice" – Her father said to her just an hour before the counselling.
"I am confident dad, but Simran told me that these days the state quota is lesser then those of the previous years, so I am not sure." – She replied

Her mother arrived by then and said to her, "Be confident and have faith in god. We should leave for the counselling centre by now, so as to reach there on time."

Her mother was quite punctual on time and could be regarded as the time manager of the family. May it be to reach the railway station on time to catch the train, or the time management to reach the exam centre before exam, she was quite careful and always ensured that the family member concerned should be on time.

AT THE COUNSELLING CENTRE

All the students were on time as they reported at the counselling centre. The counselling began and everyone was waiting for the result to be declared as per the preference form filled by the applicants.

Everyone was waiting for the allotment results. Everyone over there seemed anxious about the college allotment, just then Shruti's name was called upon. She went inside for the document verification. Her parents wanted to go but the family members were not allowed to accompany with the students inside the allotment chamber.

Shruti went to the document verification centre and her documents were verified. She got through phases and at the final place an announcement was made – "Regional Medical College allotted to Miss Shruti Singh."

Her parents also listened to the announcement and were very happy as their long term wish had come true. They thanked the god in heart.

In the allotment chamber, Shruti also got so happy but didn't want to show overly happiness. She was excited to come out and share the good news with her parents. She signed the documents and came out with joyous smile. She hugged her mother and said, "Mom, my dream has come true. Regional college seat has been allotted."

"Yes my princess, we heard the announcement outside. We are so proud of you. May all your dreams come true" – Her father said happily.

"When will you have to join the college for orientation?" – Her father asked

"Dad, they told us to join within 7 days" – Shruti replied

16

THE FIRST DAY OF COLLEGE

Shruti went on time to the college. Her mother and father were very happy as their daughter will be starting her new phase of career as a student of the prestigious regional college.

The college was a very big college made up in 3 acres and a vast campus with all the facilities like wi-fi etc. The two big gardens that consisted of green plants added a lot to the beauty of the college campus. Green cover of the college campus also excited Shruti as she was fond of the natural beauty.

In addition, security of the students was maintained by close circuit cameras and responsible guards. The principal was also an effective administrator and had a great knowledge in the field of General Surgery.

In the orientation program, the Principal told all the new students about the history of the college and the graduates and post-graduates that passed out from the college and made and were making valuable contributions to the field of Medical sciences.

Things went on very well and she got to know about various other students from different schools. The day went very nice and she was quite hopeful for her college education. She made two new friends- Simran and Manasvi.
She came to home and her mother asked her about the activities

at the college. Seeing her very happy she concluded herself that she liked the college, and was very happy.

The first day of regular classes also went well and she was enjoying the phase very well. Her performance in the class was also quite well which made a very good first impression of her in front of her teachers and the fellow students.

When the 1ˢᵗ semester exam arrived, she studied very well and all her exams went well. She was hopeful for a good result in the final exam as well as practical.

The results were out and people were surprised to learn that Shruti got the 2ⁿᵈ rank whereas the 1ˢᵗ rank was secured by Raunak, a classmate of Shruti.

Just after the results were declared, Principal called Raunak and Shruti to his chamber and congratulated them and also told them to work hard and secure good marks in the future too.

Shruti and Raunak thanked the Principal, for his kind gesture and were about to leave, when the Principal said, "I need to ask you one more thing. I hope you too can help out in this."

"Sure sir" – Raunak replied. Shruti also agreed to him.

Principal replied, "A circular has come from the governing body to conduct a debate competition in our college and then to shortlist two students for the state-level essay writing."

Raunak was very fond of writing essays and took part in essay competitions at the school level. He was excited to hear from the Principal regarding this and replied, "Yes sir. That's very good news. But what is the topic?"

"Global warming and its impact" – said the Principal.

"I am also interested to participate, sir." – Shruti replied instantly.

"Me too" – Raunak said.

The Principal got happy to see that both the toppers of the new batch are ready to take part in the competition & said, "Very nice. Two participants have already agreed to it, here itself. I will be putting out the notice on notice-board today itself."

Shruti and Raunak both were glad to know that they will be able to take part in the debate competition. For Raunak, it was a very nice opportunity to showcase his writing talent whereas for Shruti, it was her favourite topic. This was the topic on which she would love to research if given a chance to, as a hobby.

Shruti and Raunak went back to the class and attended lectures and the practical classes. Shruti came back to home after the college and was very happy for the competition but was sad because she was not able to be the No.1 in her college.

"Raunak is a random guy and how did he managed to get No.1 rank." – Shruti thought and remembered that whenever she notices him in the class or anywhere, he was talking about some cricket match or some football championship.

Before coming to home, she did look up to the notice board for the relevant details of the essay competition like words requirements, deadlines, etc.

She was excited for the essay competition and talked with her mother about it. She also told her about the result of the first semester and regretted for not being the first in her college.

"Don't be tensed. Try your best and learn from your mistakes" – Her mother said calmly.

"Yes mom. I will try to rectify the mistakes, I made in the first semester" – Shruti replied gladly.

"Yes my princess. That's the spirit" – Her mother said happily with smile on her face.

She then went to the kitchen for cooking. Shruti followed her and asked her, "Mom, I am taking part in the essay competition. If I get selected, I will get a chance to the state-level"

"Very good. I hope it will not affect your studies." – Her mother said

"No problem, mom. I will keep 1hour a day for the essay and continue on with my studies for the rest of the time." – Shruti replied

Her mother turned to her, and said, "My princess is learning to manage time these days and I am very happy to see this."

"It's all due to you, mom. Love you." – Shruti said affectionately.

"Love you too, my princess." – Her mother replied.

Days passed by and the date of the competition came. Totally, 30 students applied for it and when the results came out the best two were shortlisted – Shruti and Raunak.

Now, they both had to participate in the essay competition at the state level. Both of them were very happy. The Principal was also happy as he was confident that both the students will make the college proud at the state level.

They both had to travel to a different city for the state level competition. Raunak went to the city along with his elder brother Vivek, whereas Shruti went with her father.

"Hello Shruti, Best wishes!" – Raunak greeted her when they met at the Railway station. He also showed his regards to her father, by greeting him, which her father liked

"Who is he?" – Her father asked curiously when he went away.

"He is Raunak. He is the second participant from our college." – Shruti replied

Her father looked at her. He understood that Raunak was the

guy who got the No.1 position in the first semester examination, which made Shruti upset.

He smiled and said, "Never be tensed. Try your best and then leave the outcome to god." Both of them gave their utmost performance at the competition and were eagerly waiting for the results to be announced. They came back to their homes and started preparation for the semester exams that were set to be conducted at the end of the month.

The change that happened between them was that now they had become good friends. Shruti, who was thinking that Raunak is just a rival, had to change her feeling as she came to know that he is a quite sensible and hard working student. She was determined, that instead of being jealous of him she will try her best to score good marks not to downgrade anyone but to upgrade herself.

NEXT DAY AT THE COLLEGE

Shruti arrived the college on time and parked her scooty in the parking lot. She rushed to the Biochemistry lab as she thought, she might get late. Prof. Shukla was a strict teacher. Though, she is in his good looks but she didn't want to take any chance. When she arrived in the lab, she was surprised to know that only 2-3 students were there. Prof. Shukla had also not arrived till them

She was thinking to call Simran her best friend. She took the phone out of her bag and was about to call her, when she heard someone said - "Hello Shruti". Shruti turned around to see that it was Raunak. She smiled a bit and replied, "Hello Raunak, how are you?"
"I am fine. What about you?" – Raunak replied happily.

"I am fine too. How was your essay? I was not able to communicate with you after the competition got over." – Shruti asked

"The essay was fine. Rest it depends on the evaluator. Haha.." – Raunak chuckled.

Raunak had a great sense of humour. He was usually seen cracking jokes with his friends and it was surprising to know that he was the class topper.

"Mine was also fine. Let's see what's the result? Do you know any expected date of result of the competition?" – Shruti asked

Raunak replied - "No. But, I can guess the result. I wrote it badly. I mean I was unable to prepare for it. So, I can't say anything about it."

"Good morning class." – Prof. Shukla came to the lecture hall. Everyone went silent. Shruti turned to move to her seat, when she saw Simran rushing to her seat.

The day went as usual, as of a medico in-making. Going through the lengthy theory classes followed by lengthy practical classes was a usual schedule as everyone was used to it.

RAUNAK

Raunak was sitting along with his best friend Dhiren. Dhiren and Rahul were school time friends and had a great friendship, since then.

"So, what were you talking with the Tree's sister?" – Dhiren asked

"Tree's sister, who?" – Raunak asked curiously.

"You don't know? The girl dressed in the blue coloured salwar suit, with whom you were talking sometimes before. No.2 topper" – Dhiren responded in a puzzled way

Raunak thought for a second, and then replied – "I was talking with Shruti. Why are you calling her Tree's sister?"

17

"Every year she ties Rakhi to a Neem tree planted outside her house. She is the Tree's sister." – Dhiren answered

"What? I will confirm it from her."

"Just go and confirm. Go ahead, Raunak if you don't believe me, huh" – Dhiren answered confidently

Seeing his confidence, Raunak convinced him, "Shruti didn't mention about her brother tree. Why she ties Rakhi to a tree?

"I need to ask her and confirm this thing, at the earliest" – Raunak determined, as Prof. Shukla called his name in the attendance.

Silence occurred in the classroom.

"Raunak.. I saw him today, where has he gone now." – Prof. Shukla called the name again.

"Present sir." – Raunak responded hurriedly, realizing that the attendance is being taken.

Everyone including Prof. Shukla stared at him. Prof. Shukla looked in a complaining way but continued with taking the attendance without saying anything to him.

Prof. Shukla took the class and when the class had finished, Raunak was somehow relieved. Since the beginning of the class, he was waiting for the class to get over to ask Shruti about the Tree.

Prof. Shukla moved to the next class and then Raunak met Shruti. She was surrounded by Simran and her friends so he didn't ask her.

When she was moving out, Raunak gathered the courage to ask her, "Shruti, I need to ask you something?"

Shruti got a bit astonished but then replied, "Yes Raunak. Ask" Raunak then asked her to move out of the class away from the other people. Shruti realised it was unusual but continued with him to the outside of the classroom.

"Shruti, I need to ask you that do you tie Rakhi to a tree every Raksha bandhan?"
"Yes. It's true" - Shruti replied.

Raunak was surprised to listen that Shruti agreed to this, instantly. He thought that his friends might be playing prank with him but it was not a prank.
He further asked - "Can I know why?"

Shruti got a bit nervous on being asked so. She stood quiet for a while but then replied, "Anything that happen may not have any background reason. We like doing something and we do it. We care for someone or something and we do care. It's as simple as that."

Raunak realized that he had asked the question at the wrong time. He was just introduced to Shruti, and directly asking personal emotional questions were not correct.
He realized and said – "I am sorry."
"It's alright" – Shruti replied.

Raunak went straight away to the canteen where he sat and thought for a while. Dhiren followed him to the canteen.

Dhiren said, - "I told you that I am correct. Now, she herself confessed that she treats the tree as her brother."
Raunak was sad and replied, "Yes, you were right.
"Did she tell why?"
"No. She told that people usually develop emotions and that's it." – Raunak replied

Raunak realized that he is still not in the position of friendship where he can ask personal questions from her. He realized that in future he will abstain from asking such questions.

He went back and attended the class and after the class, he took his bag and was all set to go home.

When he reached the parking lot he saw Shruti was also in the parking lot. Shruti looked at him and then came to him.
"You wanted to know that why I tie a Rakhi to a tree?" – Shruti asked

"Yes. But only if you wish to tell" – Raunak responded and clarified his intentions that he didn't want to know anything against her wish.
"I didn't have any brother. I used to miss a brother a lot." – Shruti said.

"When my parents saw this, they taught me that trees also have lives and they also share the same relationship with nature as we have." – Shruti continued

"They encouraged me to tie Rakhi to the tree. I was hesitant to tie at first, but then I tied it happily."
"Ok. That means your parents instilled it in your mind." – Raunak concluded

"Yes, initially they motivated me for this. But, when I grew up then I realized that they were correct. The trees also have a right towards the nature that has to be ensured by us.

As human beings we are able enough to judge things and we can surely give something in return to their favour to us by combating Global warming." - Shruti added.

Raunak heard her lines but was unable to understand what to tell. He was unable to answer anything to her understanding. If we analyse things, we must be grateful to the nature and natural resources, but what we do is that we exploit these resources to our choice and never think about their protection or conservation.

"A tree can't speak like a brother does, can't play with kids like a brother does, can't do many things, but it can protect our environment, which a brother can't do." – Shruti added

"Shruti, I completely agree with all your points. These are the things, which we usually forget or say ignore. But, they need not to be ignored and should be taken care of. I am so proud to get you as a friend. Will you be my friend?" – Raunak said.

"Off course, we are friends." – Shruti replied happily.
"Ok. So, I am your friend. I need to ask you for a favour." – Raunak replied.

"Favour, Sure. Ask." – Shruti replied but was confused.
Raunak laughed and replied, "I need to meet your brother soon. I need to see it, if it is possible."

Shruti got happy and surprised to hear this, as she commonly used to get advice like to leave such things and to move on, etc.

People usually referred such things as childish.

"Offcourse. It is possible for sure. I will let you know at the earliest." Shruti replied with a smile on her face.

"That's very nice of you, Shruti." – Raunak replied reciprocating the smile.

This was the start of the friendship of the two people both of whom were quite concerned about the environment. Later on with the passage of time it developed into affection.

After the completion of their studies, Raunak and Shruti married each other with the consent of their parents.

This was a coincidence in itself, that Shruti's parents .i.e. Mr. Pramod Singh and Mrs. Indra Singh both possessing the same academic qualifications and had same deep interest in Environment and even their next gen Shruti Singh and her husband Raunak also had the same academic qualifications and deep interest in Environment and its conservation.

The foundation seed that was sown years back by Mr. And Mrs. Singh developed into a big sized tree called "Vraksh Sewa evum Samvardhan Sansthan" that is efficiently managed by Dr Shruti Singh Sisodiya and her husband Dr Raunak Sisodiya.

The tree is still there outside the Singh's house and every Rakhi, the tradition to go to brother's house and to tie Rakhi to its fist is followed by Mrs. Shruti.

Epilogue

AT THE EVENT

The event was organised by Mrs. Asthana and her businessman husband Mr. Hansraj Asthana in a top-class hotel of the city. When the car reached the venue, Mrs. Asthana was there, near the entrance gate to escort Dr. Shruti Singh Sisodiya.

When Dr. Shruti came out of the car, she warmly welcomed her and said, "Madam, I am very happy that you took time from your tight schedule for the event".
"Such events where we can express our views to such a wide audience is what I want. Awareness is the thing that can help a lot, if done the right way." – Dr. Shruti Singh replied. She was wearing a blue-pink coloured sari.

"Yes madam, that's true." – Mrs. Asthana said and then both of them came to the main hall of the entrance. After formally meeting with the other trustees and the organisers, they moved towards the stage.
"No one came from your family, ma'am, I heard that your son has arrived at home for holidays." – Mrs. Asthana asked after getting seated on the stage.

Dr. Shruti Singh kept silent for a while and then replied, "He has a school reunion today. He wanted to come, but his friends strongly insisted that he should give company to them."

This statement of her convinced Mrs. Asthana but Dr. Shruti was feeling guilty for telling a lie. Mrs. Asthana took the mike and gave her introductory speech. Dr. Shruti was watching the event but somehow she was sad how her son refused coming to the event, right away, due to the argument over the lease issue.

Mr. Hansraj Asthana announced, that he got 1000 plant saplings planted today at various public places of the city, which made everyone clap and praise him. Mr. Hansraj Asthana was the owner of a manufacturing company and he was a trustee to several non-profit organisations.
"How can he do it just because I denied the lease of the property?" – She asked to her inner self. She was in her thoughts thinking about the issue when Mrs. Asthana hinted her about her turn for the speech. She got up and took the mike in hand.

She introduced herself before the speech, and then started with the speech. "Good Evening Ladies & Gentleman, Before starting the speech I would like to introduce myself. I am Dr. Shruti Singh Sisodiya. I would like to thank Mr. and Mrs. Asthana for giving me a chance to express my views in front of you. Global Warming is an issue that is being dealt up by the whole world these days. The presence of the green house gases is the chief cause of Global warming, as you all know." – She started.

"I would like to urge to all of you that you should contribute towards the prevention of Global warming as much as possible. Governments and International Organisations are much concerned and doing their best possible in dealing with the issue but still, the general public need to be aware of this.

If we take an oath or commitment to plant a tree on every special occasion of life like birthdays, anniversary, etc, then it will help a lot. It will make our country India, a lot greener and contribute to a greener world, too. We need to give rise to the next Green Revolution in India. The ill-effects of

Global warming can be prevented to a much extent, if we take a commitment to plant trees and learn to use non-conventional energy resources.

On the extreme, if a person only plants a single plant in his/her own life and take care of it, and then also we will be able to make a green India & a greener world."

She looked at the audience and then said, "I am a responsible citizen. Be one by contributing towards a clean and green country and world. Jai Hind!" The audience clapped loudly and she ended her speech. After the speech, she managed to get an exit from the hall along with Mrs. Asthana.

"I am proud of you, mom" – Someone said from behind as she reached the entrance gate.

She turned to see that Pratik was standing with a smile on his face. Everyone walking along with her was eager to know about him. She realised it and introduced him proudly, "He is my son, Pratik. He is employed in Australia, and presently, back at home for holidays."

She had to ask various questions that arose in her mind on seeing Pratik, but she kept silent. While going to home in the car together, she could not control the urge to ask him. She asked, "You didn't go to meet your friends?"

"Mom, I postponed it to some other day. Attending this event was also important. Isn't it?" – He replied slowly.

Dr. Shruti Singh was happy on hearing this and said, "I am very happy that you came for the event."

He was about to say something when his phone rang. He took it out and it was Mr. Peter calling from Australia. Her mother kept silent. She had seen the caller's name and decided to keep silent over the issue.

He took the phone in hand, and tapped the 'Reject' option to reject the incoming call.

"It's an ISD call and that too from your boss. You could have stopped the car along the side and taken the call. Then why you didn't?" – Dr. Shruti asked him

"We are going somewhere and so I don't want to be interrupted by any

phone call." — Pratik replied.
"Where are we going? Aren't we going home?" — His mother asked.
"We have arrived at the Tree's house, mom" — Pratik responded after a while as he stopped the car at the main-gate of their ancestral house.

His mother looked at the gate and got surprised. She asked, "What did you said, whose house?"
"The Tree's house" — Pratik replied happily and showed her, the childhood-photo of her tying Rakhi to the tree. She had kept it along with the diary in the almirah.
Tears came in her eyes, as she took the photo in her hand. Those tears were the tears of happiness and gave a shining appearance to her eyes.

*****

AN APPEAL

Plant a tree and encourage others to plant trees too. Together we can lead to Green India & a greener world.

- Author

www.ingramcontent.com/pod-product-compliance
Lightning Source LLC
Chambersburg PA
CBHW020251150626
46552CB00020B/773